Trevor Holman is English and was born, brought up, and educated in South London, where he worked for many years as a professional musician before moving to Norfolk, also in the UK. For most of that time, Trevor's career was centered on music and advertising, while also serving in court as a Magistrate / Justice of the Peace.

In 2003, Trevor and his wife, Frances, moved to the Algarve in Southern Portugal, where he began a fruitful collaboration with a local lyricist, and the two of them have written in excess of one hundred songs, as well as four complete stage musicals. Trevor is now concentrating full time on his writing career and is currently working on this series of *Algarve Crime Thrillers* of which *The Faro Forger* is the second, following on from where the first in the series *The Mijas Murderer* finished. Trevor and his wife still live in the Algarve region of Southern Portugal.

To Gary Ellis, a really good friend who truly understood that a friend in need is a friend IN NEED.

Disclaimer

This novel is a work of fiction.

Names and characters used in this novel are the product of the author's imagination and any resemblance to actual persons, living or dead, is entirely coincidental.

Trevor Holman

THE FARO FORGER

The Second of the Algarve Crime Thrillers

AUSTIN MACAULEY PUBLISHERS™
LONDON • CAMBRIDGE • NEW YORK • SHARJAH

Ordering Information:
Quantity sales: special discounts are available on quantity purchases by corporations, associations, and others. For details, contact the publisher at the address below.

Publisher's Cataloging-in-Publication data
Holman, Trevor
The Faro Forger: The Second of the Algarve Crime Thrillers

ISBN 9781641821186 (Paperback)
ISBN 9781641821179 (Hardback)
ISBN 9781641821162 (E-Book)

The main category of the book — Fiction / Thrillers / Suspense

www.austinmacauley.com/us

First Published (2019)
Austin Macauley Publishers LLC
40 Wall Street, 28th Floor
New York, NY 10005
USA

mail-usa@austinmacauley.com
+1 (646) 5125767

I would like to acknowledge the support of my wonderful wife, Frances, who always encourages me in whatever crazy ideas and schemes I come up with, including the writing of this series of books.

Characters in the Book

Algarve, Portugal :

Michael Turner
Me. Murder, Mystery and Travel Writer, and part-time Police Consultant
Dr Samantha Clark
Ex Police Surgeon and now a private doctor based in Quinta do Lago
Inspector Paulo Cabrita
Portuguese GNR Officer (Police)
Cornelius Janssen
The Faro Forger

London :

Superintendent Stephen Colshaw
Metropolitan Police – based in Greenwich, South London
Detective Inspector Paul Naismith
Metropolitan Police – based in Greenwich, South London
Detective Sergeant Richard Thorpe
Metropolitan Police – based in Greenwich, South London
Sergeant Don Priestly
Metropolitan Police Desk Sergeant – based in Greenwich, South London
Clive Spencer
American Express UK Fraud Investigator

Amsterdam, Netherlands :

Commissioner Kurt Meisner
Interpol Officer – Commander in Chief (Europe)
Brigadier Helena Van Houten
Interpol Officer – Head of European Operations

Senior Inspector George Copeland
Interpol Officer – Senior Pilot and Covert Operative
Inspector Colin O'Donnell
Interpol Officer – Co Pilot and Covert Operative
Sergeant Jo Sylvester
Interpol Officer – Covert Operative

South Africa :

Martin Smith
Reformed Burglar – Interpol Officer and Specialist Covert Operative

Abu Dhabi and Dubai :

Ahmed Bukhari
Elder of two brothers
Nudara Bukhari
Younger brother and the Accountant
Jamilah Almasi
Ahmed and Nudara Bukhari's PA.
Captain Khalid Alfarsi
Dubai Police
Brigadier Murad El Hashem
Dubai Police
Brigadier Sharif Saqqaf
Abu Dhabi Police

Oman :

The Sultan of Oman
Monarch and Head of State of Oman
Major General Tariq Khan
Oman Army Ground Forces
Lieutenant Asif Hamid
Oman Army Ground Forces

Crete, Greece :

Alexio Ribeiro
The Bukhari's gang boss operating in Crete and Faro

Chapter One

Where to start? For me, that's always the most difficult aspect of writing a book. I was a reasonably successful murder and mystery writer for many years, which was how I used to earn my living, but that all changed a couple of years ago and I'm now a part-time travel and crime writer, and for the last few months I've become an official Metropolitan Police Consultant. I thought I'd start to tell you about this latest episode in my life with a brief resume of the events that took place over the last eight months or so, and shaped what was to become this – my new way of life. If you aren't already familiar with the virtually non-stop goings-on from my previous scribblings, an interesting tome in which the protagonist is now referred to as '*The Mijas Murderer*', I will try and fill you in as they say! On the assumption that you don't already know this, my name, by the way, is Michael Turner and I'm now thirty-nine years old.

I'm based in the Algarve in southern Portugal and I live in a beautiful three-bedroom villa with a swimming pool, only rented though I'm afraid, with my gorgeous fiancée Dr. Sam Clarke who runs her own private medical practice in an area of the Algarve called Quinta do Lago. This area of southern Portugal gets around 300 days of sunshine a year and I have to say, having now lived here for several years, Portugal is a fantastic country to live in.

The particular area I live in is known by most locals and visitors as the 'Golden Triangle', and it comprises of Quinta do Lago, Vale de Lobo and Vilamoura. It got its nickname for the simple reason; most of the villas around here change hands for well in excess of ten million euros, which is why I consider myself very lucky to have been able to rent my own luxury three-bedroom villa.

To cut a long story short, about eight months ago, one of my neighbors was brutally murdered during the course of a robbery at his home. Sam, who was a very experienced and well-respected Metropolitan police surgeon before moving to the Algarve, and myself got dragged into the case, and we eventually ended up working closely with the police forces of three different countries and Interpol. We travelled thousands of miles around the world acting as undercover investigators, and fortunately for us, we survived to tell the tale. Shortly after it was all over, I popped the big question and Sam agreed to marry me. We haven't set a definite date for the wedding yet, but I'm pretty sure it will be here in the Algarve sometime later this year, or maybe next?

This particular story begins very much in the way the last one did, i.e. it was a gloriously hot day in early June, and we were both sitting outside by the pool having a cup of tea and a few of my favorite bourbon biscuits when the front doorbell rang. I jumped up and made my way through the villa and opened the door to find a delivery driver from DHL.

"Meester Michael Turner," he said, elongating Mr. as a lot of Portuguese tend to do.

"That's me," I cheerfully replied.

"Ah, that is good," he said. "I have a parcel for you." And he handed me a box about twelve inches long by eight inches wide, and roughly six inches deep. It was wrapped in brown paper and sellotape, had three different labels on it, and was reasonably heavy.

Along with the parcel, he handed me his clipboard and asked me to sign alongside my name to say that I'd received the delivery. I duly did so.

"What is in the parcel and who is it from?" I asked him.

"I'm sorry Meester Michael," he replied. "I only know that it came to you from a big shop in England. Thank you. Good morning." With that, he grabbed his clipboard back, turned around, walked back to his bright yellow van with the well-known red logo and left.

I walked through the house and back out to the pool carrying my parcel and sat down.

"Who was it?" queried Sam.

"DHL delivering this parcel," I cautiously replied, "but I have absolutely no idea what it is or who on earth it could possibly be from."

"Oh no," she replied urgently. "You know what you must do now then?"

"No, what?" I stupidly asked.

"Open the wretched thing and find out," she replied laughing at me.

I made a rude face and poked my tongue out at her, then ripped off the brown paper to discover a box inside it, informing me that the contents consisted of a rather splendid, top of the range, Canon digital camera, complete with an extra telephoto lens.

"I see," said Sam, "treating yourself, yet again?"

"Not at all," I replied. "I haven't ordered a digital camera. I've already got an excellent Nikon which I love, and I have no desire to change it."

Looking at one of the labels on the brown paper, I could see the camera had been sent to me by John Lewis's Mail Order department in London, and there was a phone number for use in the event of damage to the contents or any mistakes with the delivery. I wandered back into the villa, picked up my mobile from the coffee table and dialed the number on the delivery sheet. Five minutes later, I returned to Sam by the pool.

"Well," enquired Sam, "how did you get on?"

"Apparently," I began, "I ordered the camera online about a week ago and gave them my American Express card details to pay for it. They said the card cleared and everything was correct, but as is their strict policy, they will only deliver items to the address of the cardholder rather than the address that was requested in the online transaction."

"Is that normal?" queried Sam.

"Well, according to the guy I spoke to at John Lewis, he said most companies don't have this policy, but they do, and as a result, this does occasionally happen. He also said that when there is a conflict between the requested delivery address and the card holder's address, it usually turns out that the customer's credit card has been cloned. He suggested that I should telephone American Express straight away."

"Oh, great. That's just what we need," mused Sam.

I telephoned American Express as I wandered back inside the villa, briefly explained what had happened to the girl on the switchboard, and I was then put through to a Mr. Clive Spencer in the fraud department. I gave him all my card details and repeated to him what had happened. He asked me to hold on while he went away and investigated. He then disappeared, and in the meantime blessed my ears with yet another awful recording of Vivaldi's Four Seasons. He came back on the line about six or seven minutes later.

'I'm so sorry to have kept you waiting, Mr. Turner," he said, "but it looks like John Lewis are correct and your card has been cloned. According to our records, you have used your charge card to purchase eleven top of the range digital cameras from seven different stores, and included in that were four online purchases, and all in the last five days. They have all been delivered to an address in Hackney, South London, apart from, of course, the package you received in Portugal this morning."

"Good God, eleven cameras?" I muttered. "I dread to ask, but how much has been spent using my card?" I asked.

"During the last five days Mr. Turner, your account shows spending amounting to nineteen thousand, six hundred and seventy-two pounds, and as I said, all the purchases were either in London or online," he replied.

"But I haven't even used the card in the last four days," I pleaded. "I haven't bought anything online, and I live in the Algarve in Southern Portugal which is where I have been for the last month."

"Mr. Turner," he continued, "please, don't worry. If this turns out to be fraudulent use of your card, which even at this early stage I'm pretty certain it is, you won't be charged for any of these purchases. We have insurance cover for exactly this sort of event happening."

"Well, thank God for that," I replied. "I guess this must be a big problem then if Amex has specific insurance?" I asked him.

"It is, and all the card companies have to hold insurance cover, Mr. Turner. Would you believe there are now over thirty million credit cards in circulation, and over ninety-five million debit cards, half of which are contactless?"

"I'm sorry to take up your time, Mr. Spencer, but if you don't mind me asking, how does cloning work?"

'It works very well, actually. Sorry, Mr. Turner, just my little joke. How does it work? Well, years ago, when this first became a problem, crooked traders would usually clone the card in the shop where they worked. The usual procedure was to have two scanners, one the legal one registered to the shop, and a second illegal one they'd got on the black market which was used simply to steal the card information. Importantly for the crooks, both scanners would always be positioned out of your sight line. They would swipe your card firstly in the illegal machine, apologize and say something like the swipe didn't work properly, and then they'd swipe your card again, but this time in the legal device located just behind the illegal one. Your card has then been cloned, and you know absolutely nothing about it."

"You make it sound so simple. But surely, Mr. Spencer, companies like yours have ways of preventing this illegal cloning built into the cards."

"Oh we do, and over the years we keep adding more and more protection. But as fast as we improve the protection, the crooks improve ways of getting around it. Nowadays, for example, crooks can use hi-tech hacking units to fund their shopping sprees using the stolen card details, and that's what I suspect has happened with your charge card. As I said, these days the hacker can skim details from any credit, debit, or charge card of people by simply standing next to them."

"You mean they don't even have to touch your card?" I asked.

"That's right," he replied. "These new 'skimmers' as they're called can read any bank card from roughly three inches away. The thief just has to get close enough to your pocket where you think your card is safely tucked away, nice and secure in your wallet, and they just press a switch on the device in their pocket. These new skimmers will read 1,024 bytes of electronic information per second, which to the layman is the equivalent to copying the details of fifteen bank cards per second."

"But what do they do with all the information?" I asked him. "Surely they need the actual card in their possession to go on a shopping spree as you called it."

"No, not at all. They can capture the encrypted data, extracting the card's number and even the holder's name, address, and a mini-statement in some cases. That's all they need, particularly if they use the information to shop online. The big crooked outfits also have massive stocks of pre-printed blank cards that contain no information until your details are electronically added. They can then take what to all intents and purposes is your card and go on a short spending spree in any shop that accepts that particular card."

"OK, I now get that and accept it, but why on earth would they want to buy eleven digital cameras?" I asked. "Surely, whoever did this can't love photography that much."

"Correct Mr. Turner. They're not in the least bit interested in taking photographs. They simply sell the cameras on the black market. Top end hi-tech equipment is incredibly easy to shift. So, it could be digital cameras, laptops, notebooks, tablets, smartphones etc. Look, let's say for example they've bought fifteen, top of the range digital cameras costing fifteen hundred pounds each, using your charge card. They then sell the cameras on, for say three hundred pounds each. The thieves have made a whopping four thousand five hundred quid for doing bugger all. Sorry about the language, by the way."

"Oh, don't worry," I replied. "I've felt like swearing ever since I found out about this."

"Look, as I said earlier, please don't worry, Mr. Turner. I have already put a stop on your old card and issued you with a new charge card today. Unfortunately, having your card cloned or skimmed is one of the problems of having a card like yours with no limit on it. They attract the thieves who know they can go on a quick spending spree, make several grand and then move on somewhere else, burning the card before they get caught using it."

"Well, thank you for all your time and your explanations, Mr. Spencer. Is there anything else you need from me at the moment?"

"Just one thing, Mr. Turner. I suspect your card was cloned somewhere in London. I see from our records of your purchases that you were in Greenwich in South London not that long ago. I think it must have happened there, and I was wondering if you can think of where your card might have been swiped during that time."

"Offhand, no I can't," I replied. "But I'll certainly give it some thought."

"Well thank you, Mr. Turner. I'm sorry this has happened to you, but please don't worry and feel free to ring me anytime if you can think of any information that may help the fraud department. In the meantime, your new card should be delivered to you by a registered courier within the next couple of days."

"Thank you for all your help, Mr. Spencer. Goodbye," and I put the phone down.

I returned to the poolside, poured another cup of tea as my first one had gone cold, and repeated everything I'd discussed with Clive Spencer to Sam. We chatted it over for a few minutes and then Sam suddenly said, "I know where it happened. It was in the bar of that hotel we went for a drink one evening, you know, with Stephen and Paul in Greenwich."

Stephen was Superintendent Stephen Colshaw of the Metropolitan Police, and Paul was Inspector Paul Naismith of the same esteemed organization. Both of them operated out of Greenwich Police station, and we'd all worked closely together on the Mijas Murderer case.

"Do you remember that barman," continued Sam. "He swiped your card twice saying the first time hadn't worked, and then he showed you a bit of paper saying 'failed swipe', which he then tore it up and threw in the bin. As Mr. Spencer said, we couldn't see the machine he was using behind the bar, and I wouldn't mind betting he's got a whole pile of 'failed swipe' bits of paper back there alongside an illegal second machine."

"You're right Sam. I bet it was that bastard."

"I suggest you ring back Clive Spencer, and he can put his fraud people onto it."

"Yeah, right. Along with the fifty thousand other frauds they're currently investigating. No, I want to see the color of that bloody barman's eyes. Pack your bags, Sam. We're going on a little trip back to Greenwich."

Chapter Two

We packed, drove to Faro airport, left my most prized possession parked there – an Italian racing red Jaguar XF with an ivory leather interior, and caught a late afternoon flight to London Gatwick. From there, we took the Gatwick Express into Central London and then a local train from Charing Cross to Greenwich. By the time we arrived, it was too late to do anything other than check into our hotel. We'd decided not to book ourselves into the hotel where the cloning had happened, but instead we went to our favorite hotel in this part of the world, the new fivestar InterContinental near the O2 arena. It was quite expensive and on the previous occasion we'd stayed there, Interpol had been paying. But after what had happened, we felt we deserved a bit of luxury. We had a very nice meal in the hotel's restaurant, and then as it was only ten o'clock, we couldn't resist paying a visit to the hotel bar where we suspected my card had been cloned.

We walked into the bar, and both noticed straight away that neither of the two bar staff on duty was the man I was looking for. I knew that in most hotels the bar staff come under the authority of the restaurant's Maître d', and so that's where we headed next.

"I'm so sorry to disturb you," I began. "I can see you're closing down for the evening, but I wonder if you can help us."

"We were looking for one of your barmen," said Sam. "A tall man with short sandy colored hair. He served us a few weeks ago and we'd like a word with him."

"Don't tell me," replied the Maître d'. "He skimmed your credit card and you want to give him a black eye."

"Yeah, something like that," I replied.

"I'm so sorry about your card Mr.…?" he asked.

"Turner, Michael Turner."

"Ooh, you're not 'the' Michael Turner are you? The famous author?"

"Well, I don't know about being famous," I replied.

Although secretly I was really pleased to have had my name recognized, and to be called 'the' Michael Turner, well that was the icing on the cake. Anyway, I knew Sam could see the pleasure on my face as she was smiling gently to herself.

"But yes," I continued. "I have written a few successful murder mysteries in my time. Thank you. Now, about your barman."

"Oh yes, Mr. Turner. Sorry, but we don't get many true celebrities in here. Anyway, the barman you're looking for is a Donald Preston. Well, at least that's the name he gave us. As soon as we found out what he was doing we sacked him and reported it straight away to the police station down the road."

"Can you remember whom you spoke to there?" I asked him.

"No, not off hand, I haven't a clue. No, I tell a lie. He gave me his card. I've got it here somewhere in my drawer, I think."

The Maître d' slid open his desk drawer and rifled through a thick wad of business cards.

"Yes, this is it," he said. "An Inspector Paul Naismith."

Sam and I just looked at each other and smiled. We thanked the Maître d' who turned out to have a far more down-to-earth and very 'un-French' name than his title might suggest. He was, in fact, Mr. Colin Peacock who lived in Deptford, one of the seedier areas of South London. We left and returned to the InterContinental, had a drink during which we decided to visit Inspector Paul Naismith in the morning, and then turned in for the night.

After breakfast, we decided a walk to Greenwich Police Station would do us both good, but I have to say, by the time we got there I wished we hadn't.

I was well and truly knackered. If I'm being perfectly honest, I don't do a lot of exercise in the Algarve. Most of the time I'm sitting on my backside, either at the PC on my desk or at my laptop by the pool, bashing out whatever the next book happens to be about. If Sam and I go out in the evening or at weekends, we usually take my Jaguar, or on rare occasions, we might use Sam's white C class Mercedes. The walk from the InterContinental to the police station was the most exercise I'd had in months, and didn't I know it? We hadn't telephoned to say we were coming to the police station, but we were lucky and the Desk Sergeant on reception told us Paul was in. He rang through and Paul came out from his office into the reception area and greeted us like two old friends, which of course we now were.

"God, it's great to see you both," he said, hugging and kissing Sam for all he was worth. Paul then turned to me, looked at me as if to say, 'Oh, you're here as well', then he smiled and gave me a hug as well and said, "You too, you lucky old sod."

I assumed he was referring to my now being engaged to Sam. Paul had always fancied Sam when she was a police surgeon, but I was the lucky one she'd decided to settle down with.

"And what brings you two to sunny London town?" Paul asked.

"Well obviously, to see me!" came a loud voice from behind us, and Superintendent Stephen Colshaw arrived in the reception area from his office. The Desk Sergeant knew Stephen would want to know we were here, and he'd phoned through to him.

"Come through to my office," he said. "You too Paul. I presume our two visitors from Portugal have got themselves into a massive spot of trouble again, which only the cream of the Metropolitan police can get them out of."

"I tell you what, Stephen," said Sam laughing. "It's a good job you're not in the least bit big-headed. That door to your office is only three-foot wide you know."

"Come in, the pair of you," Stephen smiled. "It's really good to see you both again. Pot of tea and some bourbon biscuits is the usual fare of choice, if I remember right?" said Stephen.

"I'll deal with that," Paul said as he picked up the phone and rang the canteen.

We chatted about life in general since we'd last seen Stephen and Paul at our engagement party in the Algarve, and once the tea and biscuits had arrived, we got down to the main reason for our visit. I explained to them both about what had happened with my Amex card and my apparently having bought eleven digital cameras, and then how we'd traced the cloning of my card back to the now disappeared barman at the hotel bar down the street.

"I remember that crooked little bastard," began Paul. "But he'd well and truly done a bunk and disappeared by the time I got to the hotel. We never could find him as he'd given his employers at the hotel – what turned out to be – a false name and a non-existent address. I'm really sorry, Michael."

"Do you know, cloning and skimming," said Stephen, "are now two of the biggest and most profitable types of identity theft, or fraud if you prefer, that now exist, and I'm not just talking about the UK. It really has become a world-wide problem."

"Did you know?" asked Paul, not really expecting us to reply, "that there are now at least twelve areas of forgery depending on how you categorize it. Thieves, crooks, gangs, whatever you want to call them, can and do now forge everything you can think of."

"Ah, I remember the good old days you know," said a thoughtful Stephen. "When I was a young Sergeant based in the Old Kent Road."

We all went "Aah" together and laughed. Stephen ignored us and simply continued.

"A signed bank draft in your hand was just as good as having cash in your pocket. Nowadays though, bank drafts are getting forged all the time."

"'Well, how can that work?' asked Sam. "Surely, a quick phone call to the bank manager to check if they've issued the bank draft would stop any thief in their tracks."

"Not if another member of the gang is in the bank manager's house pointing a gun at his wife," chipped in Paul. "Usually, the forger is just one member of a gang, and remember, the top gangs these days are a tight-knit team of specialists, with the forger being just one of those specialists. The others are usually brilliant drivers, excellent shots, a highly plausible and likeable frontman, a couple of top muscle men, a creative strategist, a great planner and administrator, etc."

"God, you make these gangs sound like top blue-chip companies," I said.

"To be honest, Michael, in their world, that's just what they are," continued Paul. "And top of the range forgers are one of the most sought-after people in their business. Thank God though, really good forgers are very few and far between."

"A top forger," continued Stephen taking over again, "frequently operates in several different countries, and the EU has made it so much easier now for the cash counterfeiters, or forgers if you prefer. In the good-old-days, French Francs were only really any good for you in France, but no earthly use at all in Germany where you needed the good old German Deutschmark, or Pesetas in Spain, Lire in Italy, and Escudos in Portugal etc. Nowadays, once you've made a set of good Euro plates, you can use the counterfeit notes in any EU country without people batting an eyelid."

"You mentioned forged bank drafts just now, Stephen," said Sam. "I understand about the holding the manager's wife at gunpoint bit, but just how does that work and what do the gangs do with bank drafts?"

"Well mostly they'll go after really expensive purchases," replied Stephen. "Such as the top of the range cars; Rolls Royces, Bentleys, Ferraris, Aston Martins, Lamborghinis etc. paying for them using counterfeit bank drafts. The usual procedure is to use another very important member of any criminal team, their very believable front man, who is usually a highly experienced and extremely likeable con artist. He is the team member that will set up the supposed sale over a couple of meetings the week before."

"During the second conversation for example," chipped in Paul, "they casually check that the dealer will accept a bank draft as full payment, and they then agree to complete the sale around three o'clock the following day."

"That's very important," said Stephen.

"Sorry, but why is the time important?" asked Sam.

"Because the bank will still be open at three o'clock," said Stephen, "and the car salesman will know he will be able to check the authenticity of the bank draft."

"On the day though," said Paul taking over again, "The front man will usually phone the car dealer about 02:45 p.m. to say he is sorry, but he's stuck in a meeting which has over-run and therefore he is going to be a bit late, and he then tips up with the forged bank draft once he knows the bank that supposedly issued it has closed. He presents his beautifully forged bank draft, knowing the car dealer can't check it by ringing the bank, even if he wanted to. He casually drops into the conversation that he is really looking forward to driving the car to Dover on his way to the ferry, which he still hopes he can catch on time, and then on to France. The salesman doesn't want to lose such a big sale, and it's either now or never as the man is leaving the country, and he's made sure through conversation that the dealer knows that, so he usually lets them leave with the car they are purchasing. After all, the dealer's always got insurance if anything should go wrong!"

"Quite frankly," said Stephen. "It simply wouldn't occur to nine out of ten car dealers that the really nice man they've been dealing with all this time is a top-class crook."

"The gang," said Paul taking over the story again. "Then sell whatever it is they've nicked to a pre-arranged customer, usually in another country, or they fence it before the bank opens the next day. In the case of cars, the plates are usually changed within half an hour of the sting, they're then driven straight onto a ferry at Dover, Harwich, Portsmouth or Plymouth."

"Sometimes," said Stephen, "they'll take the car to Ireland first, to throw us off the scent, and then take it immediately out again and into Europe from there."

"Nine times out of ten, the cars have disappeared inside Europe before the dealer even knows he's been had," said Paul finishing the story.

"Exactly the same thing happens with jewelry," said Stephen. "The deal is carefully set up in a classy and exclusive jewelry shop in the same way as the car scenario."

"They will always use a top-class front person," confirmed Paul, "Or in the case of jewelry it's usually a very personable man and woman team playing the loving happy couple. On the day they will always arrive late, present the forged bank draft, take the goodies and disappear. It's big business."

"You said earlier Stephen," I muttered in between a mouthful of biscuits, "that there are twelve areas of forgery. If you don't mind me asking, what are they?"

I think they'd been waiting for that question as Stephen and Paul's double act then kicked into top gear.

"Well firstly there are the obvious things such as 'Currency'. I'm including in that counterfeit notes, very rarely but occasionally coins, cheques, and bank drafts as we've just been talking about."

"Then there are 'Bonds'," said Paul, "which are similar to currency in that they can be used illegally to raise money."

"There are 'Promissory Notes'," said Stephen, "which are fairly self-explanatory as are 'Money Orders'."

“Forged ‘Deeds’ are also an extremely good source of income,” chipped in Paul, “in that the crooks will pretend to own something they don’t by showing the purchaser, or perhaps I should call him the mug, a set of forged deeds.”

“They will then exchange the forged deeds for money,” said Stephen.

“Usually offering a much better deal if the buyer can pay in cash, usually suggesting they already pay the tax man too much.”

Paul then took over the list.

“‘Corporate Documents’ work in a similar way to deeds, but this usually occurs in the world of business, where someone thinks he has bought a company for example, because he has paid for the company, mostly via an international bank transfer in exchange for either the corporate documents of the company or certified share certificates, both of which will have been cleverly forged. Quite often in this scenario, an office will be needed to ‘complete the deal’ with the client being invited to collect the deeds or shares from their solicitor’s office or from their accountant. In this type of con, the team have usually taken over a genuine office while the solicitor whose office it really is has gone to lunch.”

“That sounds a bit risky,” I said. “What happens if he returns early from lunch?”

“Oh, he won’t,” replied Stephen. “Another member of the team, usually a very attractive lady will ingratiate herself with him, and will end up inviting herself to join him for lunch. Her job is then to keep him there until she receives a text message giving the all clear to let him return from lunch.”

“The money then quickly disappears,” continued Paul, “in a series of international bank transfers into numbered accounts via numerous countries such as the Cayman Islands, the Bahamas, Lichtenstein, Switzerland etc., although not so much Switzerland nowadays, since the Swiss banks were forced to open their books.”

“‘Bills of Lading’ are quite popular on the forgery front,” said Stephen, “particularly with arms dealers who stick ten crates of ‘machine parts’ on a ship’s forged bill of lading, when in reality the ship is carrying three crates of machine parts and seven crates of Kalashnikovs.”

“Then of course there are ‘Titles’,” said Paul.

"What?" queried Sam. "You mean, Lord, Baron, Marquis, Viscount etc."

"Exactly," said Paul. "It's amazing what you can obtain as a titled person that is simply not available to us mere commoners."

"Such as?" I asked. "I'm sorry, but I don't get it?"

"Well entry into places you would otherwise be excluded from," said Stephen. "Let me give you a simple example. Let's say the Tutankhamun exhibition is coming to the British Museum next month, and before you ask, no it's not really coming. I'm just making this up. But assuming it was true, obviously nobody would be granted admission to that part of the museum prior to its official opening for the very obvious security reasons."

"But if you and your extremely elegant female accomplice," said Paul looking at Sam, "Turned up at the British Museum the day before the exhibition opened, and told them you were Lord and Lady Carnarvon, and it was your great grandfather that discovered the original tomb with Howard Carter back in nineteen whenever, and what's more, you could prove your title by showing the curator your passport in that name, complete with your title, a driving license, and a wallet full of credit cards all saying Lord Carnarvon for example, the mere fact of your title means the curator would probably give you a private tour there and then, during which you could see where all the pressure pads and laser beams were located."

"Let's be frank," said Stephen, "Knowing most museum curators, who in my humble opinion mostly live on another planet of ancient dusty relics, they'd probably tell you all about the security systems they've put in place simply out of pride."

"If, however," continued Paul, "You'd turned up as plain old Fred and Cynthia Bloggs and had your passport and driving license just the same, you'd undoubtedly be shown the door. It's the title that makes all the difference."

"Another fun area that the best gangs, and by that, I mean the most efficient and successful gangs exploit through high quality forgery," said Stephen, "is what are known as 'Bills of Exchange'."

"And what the hell are they?" I asked.

'Well," began Paul, "they're a bit complicated to explain, but basically a bill of exchange is a non-interest-bearing written order, which is used primarily in international trade. They bind one party to pay a fixed sum of money to another party, and always at a predetermined future date. I suppose you could say bills of exchange are very similar to cheques and promissory notes in that sense. They can be drawn by individuals or banks, and they are generally transferable by endorsements. The main difference between a promissory note and a bill of exchange is that the bill is completely transferable, and it can therefore bind one party to pay a third party that was not even involved in its creation. If these bills are issued by a bank, they can be referred to as bank drafts, which we talked about earlier. If they are issued by individuals, they are usually referred to as trade drafts."

"What you both need to understand," said Stephen, "is that anything manufactured or printed by anyone, anywhere can be forged and used for financial gain. Just look at the market in fake watches, fake handbags, fake shoes, fake perfume, fake anything. If it's fake, then it's basically a forgery."

"Take for example your American Express charge card," said Paul. "Yours was neatly skimmed here in Greenwich, and then used to buy several very expensive cameras online. But from what you say, they also bought cameras in shops all over London, and for that they would have had to use a physical card. That means whoever ended up with your card details simply put the information onto a pre-printed Amex card and then went on their shopping spree."

"You say you didn't get the guy that skimmed Michael's card?" Sam asked.

"No," said Paul. "He was long gone when I got to the hotel."

"I suspect," said Stephen. "He was just a collector."

"What's one of those?" asked Sam.

"A collector," said Paul, "simply sets up somewhere in a 'high traffic' area, i.e. somewhere there will be lots of transactions. That could be a bar, a shop, a ticket booth etc., anywhere where people can pay with a card. They then simply 'collect' information by illegally swiping or skimming customer's credit cards, debit cards or charge cards. Collectors don't actually do anything with the information themselves, but simply pass the details from their scanners on to whoever they're working for, usually for an agreed fee of say £500 for every ten cards. They will usually set up shop for a week, get paid their set fee by the gang they work for, and then move on to scam another group of innocents somewhere else."

"To be frank," said Stephen, "most of the time these people are in and out again, having got their information before we even know they've arrived. There's very little we can do to catch them, and all I can say is thank God the card companies have insurance that protects their customers from fraudulent use of their card."

"I'm sorry if this sounds bad," said Paul. "But the guys who skim credit cards are really small fry in the grand scheme of things. The people we really want are the top-quality forgers who through their undoubted skill and work can produce millions of counterfeit pounds or euros over a weekend."

"It's really funny that you two have turned up here today," said Stephen.

"And why is that, O Wise One, pray tell?" replied Sam.

"Well there are only five of these really top forgers Paul was describing in the world as far as we know," said Stephen.

"Now we can't be a hundred percent sure of this, but we think one of these top five forgers is located in your part of the world, and as such he is nicknamed 'the Faro Forger'."

Chapter Three

"You're joking, right?" I exclaimed. "One of the world's top forgers, based in Faro?"

"Yes, we think so," replied Stephen.

"Look, as it happens I was going to telephone you two later this week, but as you're here now I might as well ask you face to face. How do you fancy joining us again and doing a bit more undercover work?"

"I have to ask Stephen," said Sam. "Why us?"

"To be honest Sam, three reasons. One – you both know the Algarve. Two – you fit together well and are very believable. People will readily accept you for whoever you happen to say you are."

"You both proved that time and time again," said Paul. "In South Africa, Spain, Amsterdam, Venice and the Bahamas."

"And three?" I queried.

"Three," repeated Stephen, "you're both bloody good at it. You've both got a nose for sniffing out information, your instincts are good, and there's nobody I trust more."

"I make that, three, four, five and six," laughed Sam.

"So, are you up for it or not?" asked Stephen.

"Well I am," I said. "And judging by the smile on my wife to be's face, so is she."

"Great, well in that case can you both come back here tomorrow, and we'll get Richard to put a presentation together on who and what we're after. By the way, Kurt's been promoted after the Mijas job. He's left South Africa and is now the big chief of all Interpol in Europe. Although Interpol's HQ is in Lyon, Kurt decided to base himself in the Amsterdam office, and he appointed Helena as his number two and Head of Operations. As this is, in my opinion another very large and significant international problem, I'll ask them to fly over and join us for tomorrow's meeting if at all possible, but if not, we'll have to get them on a TV conference call."

"I'm in Crown Court in the morning, Stephen," said Paul, "giving evidence in the Matheson case. Any chance we can set this up for the afternoon?"

"Oh, yes, I'd forgotten that. OK Paul. Well in that case let's make it 2:00 p.m. on the dot if that's OK with you two, and hopefully it gives Kurt and Helena more time to get here."

We arrived back at Greenwich police station at 1:55 p.m. the following day, where we found both Kurt and Helena talking to Paul in the reception area.

"My God, you get uglier every day," said Kurt beaming at me.

"Yeah, and you're fatter than ever you old fart," I retorted, and with that we shared a giant 'man hug' or whatever it is they call it these days. Meanwhile, Sam and Helena were hugging each other as if their lives depended on it, when Stephen walked in.

"Any chance I can join in this love fest?" he asked.

"Of course, Stephen," smiled Helena. "But shouldn't you and I do it in the privacy of your office?"

"Oh, if only," sighed Stephen, and then we all laughed.

"You lot do all know this is supposed to be a working police station," said Don Priestly, the Desk Sergeant, using his sternest voice.

"This is where we deal with serious crimes and hardened criminals, you know. It is not an episode of Celebrity Big Brother!" He then smiled at us all.

"We consider ourselves all suitably chastised thank you Donald," laughed Stephen.

"Come on, let's all head into my office and get down to business. Paul, can you get Richard to join us, and can you also please order some tea and biscuits for everyone?"

We all sat round Stephen's conference table, and it was strange, each of us automatically took the same seats we had sat in a few months earlier when we were working on the Mijas Murderer affair. Richard, Stephen's senior tech guy, joined us, giving us outsiders a hug, and took his usual position behind two laptops, both linked to the giant TV screen on the far wall. Paul then began the meeting.

"This all started nearly two years ago when a wodge of counterfeit twenty pound notes turned up at the O2 arena. They had been used to buy tickets for an Elton John concert that were selling for between seventy and one hundred and fifty pounds each."

"Good God," said Kurt. "I wouldn't that pay much that to listen to Elton bloody John."

"Oh, come on Kurt," retorted Sam. "I loved Crocodile Rock, and Goodbye Yellow Brick Road was an absolutely brilliant album. There wasn't a duff track on it."

"No, Funeral for a Friend was a bit dire, and no way to start an album," I said.

"Er, excuse me," said Stephen, "but if 'Juke Box Jury' has finished dissecting the vocal prowess of Mr. Reginald Kenneth Dwight, can we please get back to counterfeit twenty pound notes."

"Who's Reginald Kenneth Dwight, and what on earth has he got to do with this?" muttered Helena.

"Reginald Kenneth Dwight is Elton John's real name," I replied.

"Oh," she said. "That poor man. No wonder he changed it."

"That's nothing," I said. "You wouldn't believe some of the real names of music and film stars. For example, would you believe David Bowie's real name was David Robert Hayward Stenton Jones."

"I knew that," said Stephen. "But did you know that Cher's real name is Cherilyn Sarkisian La Piere?"

"As it happens," I replied. "I did. How about Vanilla Ice then?" I asked.

"Robert Van Winkle," shot back Stephen.

"You are joking?" queried Sam. "Vanilla Ice's real name is Robert Van Winkle?"

"Sure is," I confirmed.

"People in the entertainment business," said Stephen, "have always changed their real names for various reasons. For example; Wladziu Lee Valentino became Liberace, Barry Manilow was christened Barry Alan Pincus, and Dean

Martin started out as Dino Paul Crocetti. Can you imagine any of them making it to the top with those names?"

"Freddie Mercury of Queen," I said not wishing to be outdone, "was christened Farrokh Bulsara and George Michael would you believe started life as Yorgos Panayiotou."

"Ooh, I know one," said Sam jumping up and down in her seat and raising her hand like a schoolgirl. "Cliff Richard's real name is Harry Rodger Webb."

"Well done, Sam," said Stephen, slightly mocking her. "But did you know that Dusty Springfield's real name was Mary Isabel Catherine Bernadette O'Brien?"

"No, I didn't," said Sam, "But how come you two smart Alecs know all these names?"

"Well I got interested," began Stephen, "when I was watching the film Zulu, and I read in a review that Michael Caine's real name was Maurice Micklewhite, and I wondered who else had changed their name, and why? What about you Michael?"

"Similar really I suppose." I replied. "I read somewhere that Tom Cruise was in reality named Thomas Mapother the fourth. Well that set me off, and I then discovered all sorts of wonderful name changes. Tony Curtis was really Bernard Schwartz, Doris Day's real name was Doris von Kappelhoff, and Ben Kingsley, the star of Ghandi was really Krishna Banji."

"I suppose my two favorites," said Stephen, "were two of the old Hollywood stars. Cary Grant was christened Archibald Leach. Now there's a romantic name for a leading man. Can you imagine it? 'North by North West' starring 'Archibald Leach.' But I suppose my favorite, and the best of the lot was that rugged star of numerous westerns, John Wayne, whose real name was in fact Marion Morrison."

Kurt coughed very loudly from his end of the table. "Are we all done now gentlemen, fascinating though it has been? Any chance of you English getting back to some actual police work. I believe, Stephen, you were talking about tickets to see Reginald Kenneth Dwight."

"Sorry, Kurt. Yes I was, and as I was saying before Michael so rudely interrupted me."

Stephen looked at me as he said it, and then laughed. He continued. "On a serious note, a large quantity of counterfeit twenty-pound notes was used to purchase tickets at the O2, and in total, they shifted nearly one hundred and twenty thousand pounds worth of dud money in just three days."

"Now we suspect," said Paul, "that two of the O2's temporary ticket staff were passing them out in change for anyone paying in cash. We're also pretty sure that they were also changing the counterfeits for real cash they'd both taken during the day behind the box office prior to banking the day's takings that evening in the bank's night safe. Naturally, the bank checks all notes coming in, and the counterfeit money was soon discovered once it had been banked at the end of day three, but sadly by that time, our two suspect ticket sales staff had disappeared and were never seen or heard of again."

"Then eight months ago," said Stephen, "we got a report of counterfeit ten and twenty-pound notes turning up in various antique and fine art dealers right across South East London. Now, this is one of several types of business that are referred to by Customs and Excise as high-value dealers."

"Other business categories in this class, i.e., handling a lot of cash," said Paul, "include motor dealers, motor auctioneers, jewelers, boat dealers, builders, bathroom and kitchen suppliers and general auctioneers."

"What's more," said Stephen, "businesses such as auctioneers and yacht brokers may never own most of the goods they sell, but if they receive high-value cash payments for them then they are still classed as high-value dealers, and these are the obvious targets for the counterfeiters. So we thought we'd have a ring round to a few other areas in the UK and have a word on the quiet to see if there were large amounts of counterfeit cash turning up via HVD's."

"That's high-value dealers," said Paul seeing the blank look on Helena's face.

"Sorry both," smiled Helena. "It is an abbreviation and term we do not use in Holland."

"We got a lot of information fed back to us," said Stephen, "from various areas around the country, and the first was from the Newcastle force where they had gone through a similar experience as that of the O2 at 'the Sage', a large concert venue in Gateshead."

“We then heard back from ‘the Stables’ in Milton Keynes,” said Paul, “which is another large venue, and they’d had the same problem. By the time all the calls and emails had come back to us, there were forty-three different venues that had been affected around the country, with over £2.7 million in counterfeit tens and twenties having been passed or laundered through these venues. Add to that the money dumped on the other HVD companies we mentioned earlier, and spread around the country, and we estimate that this gang has changed about five or six million pounds sterling of their lousy counterfeit money into real cash. And that’s just the deals we know about in this country. We’re pretty certain they’ve been operating all over Europe, and for all we know in the States, Australia, the Middle East, anywhere and in any currency.”

“Plus,” said Stephen taking over again, “we reckon they accomplished it all in less than two months. As a result, we feel confident that several conclusions can now be drawn.

One.

There is a gang of at least ten full-timers working in this country.

Two.

They have taken on at least sixty or seventy grunts to do the day to day spade work.”

“I’m so sorry Stephen,” said Kurt. “What, or who are ‘grunts’? This is not a word I am familiar with in South Africa.”

“Or in Holland,” said Helena.

“Sorry guys,” said Paul. “We do tend to have a habit of slipping into English criminal slang occasionally. Grunts are the workers that do all the hard graft, day after day, usually being paid peanuts. Not actual peanuts you understand, but…

“We get it Paul, thank you,” jumped in Kurt.

“Anyway, they got their nickname because in most cases the grunts were usually at the back of the queue when God was dishing out brain cells and that invariably means that instead of holding intelligent conversations, they just make the occasional grunting noise. Hence Grunts.”

“Not a very kind description, but nevertheless accurate I fear,” commented Stephen.

“To continue.

Three.

In order to have this much counterfeit cash to shift, they must have a very large and efficient printing facility somewhere.

Four.

Having seen for myself the high quality of the counterfeit cash they're producing, they must have an absolutely brilliant forger on their books to make the printing plates.

Five.

As I said to everyone earlier, there are we believe only five master forgers, as we are calling them, in the world capable of doing this high quality of work, and fortunately, at this precise moment in time we know exactly where four of them are."

"So where are these four then, and more importantly, where is the one that would seem to be the man we want?" asked Kurt.

"Richard, can you please put the relevant photographs on the screen as we go through the list," asked Stephen.

"Of course," replied Richard with fingers poised over his two laptops.

"Scott Freeman," said Paul, "is an American, and he is the number five on our list. He is currently serving year five of a fourteen-year sentence for forging hundred-dollar plates, and he can now be found residing in the salubrious US Penitentiary in Tucson, Arizona."

"Krasimir Goossens," said Stephen, "is a Belgian, and he is number four on our list. He is also inside at the moment, and he is currently serving the second year of a ten year stretch at Lantin Prison, near Liège in Belgium."

"Number three on our list is from your old part of the world Kurt," said Paul.

"Really?" exclaimed a surprised Kurt. "I wasn't aware we had a top-quality forger in South Africa. I knew about Jordi Peterssohn and Stefan Julesberg of course, but neither they nor their work is top quality. I never considered either of them to be at the top of the tree."

'No, they're not," confirmed Paul. "Our number three is a gentleman who goes by the name of Eugene Oosthuizen. Although he's South African by birth, you probably haven't come across him because he has spent the last twenty years churning out counterfeit euro plates in Hong Kong. He was caught last year when a shipment of dodgy euros on their way to Poland was intercepted en-route, and Eugene was later given up by the gang that employed him to make the plates, in exchange for lighter sentences for themselves. Eugene is now spending the next six years with his co-conspirators in Montelupich Prison in Krakow, Poland."

"The number two on our list," said Stephen, "is an elderly British gentleman who goes by the truly inspiring name of Alan Brown. Sadly for Mr. Brown, he decided not to retire at sixty-five, which is a pity for him as he contracted a mild form of Parkinson's disease which produced a very slight occasional shake in his hands. On his last job, his employers failed to check the quality of his work, and his Parkinson's well and truly dropped them all in it. They were all discovered when one of the gang was caught trying to pass counterfeit in a high-class jeweler's shop in Manchester. The smart and very brave salesman spotted a small scratch mark on the notes which shouldn't have been there, he realized the money wasn't legit, and smiled at his customer while pressing a hidden button. That dropped the bulletproof screen down, thereby protecting all the staff, and at the same time the screen dropped it automatically set off the alarms and electronically locked the doors. The police soon arrived, and took him away where he sang like a canary. The whole lot of them, including Alan Brown, were later rounded up and they are now serving various terms in prisons dotted around the UK."

"OK Stephen," I said. "You've kept us all waiting this long. So who is the world's number one counterfeiter?"

"I haven't a clue," he replied, and just sat back in his chair smiling at us.

Chapter Four

“I’m sorry,” said Sam, completely aghast. “Do you mean to say you’ve had us all sitting here through all your waffling about counterfeiting, forgery and fakes etc. and when we get to the really interesting bit, all you can say is ‘I don’t have a clue’?”

“If we knew who he was, we’d go and arrest him, wouldn’t we?” asked Paul with a very quizzical look on his face.

“Well, you didn’t arrest the Simpsons to start with, and you knew who they were right from the beginning,” I replied realizing immediately what I’d just said.

‘And why didn’t we arrest them right at the beginning?’ asked Paul looking directly at Sam and me.

“Because you had no evidence,” said a deflated looking Sam.

‘Exactly,” said Stephen leaning forward onto the conference table. “We need evidence to put him or her away, whoever they are. But not only does evidence get us a conviction, it also helps us find a name, and once we’ve got a name we usually get a picture, and once we’ve got a picture, we all know whom we’re looking for and that usually leads to us finding some decent evidence. Then we’ll get a conviction.”

“Sorry, Stephen,” I said, interrupting his flow, “you said him or her. I don’t know why, but I just assumed forgers were always men. You think this one might be a woman?”

“As I said, I haven’t a clue. There have been some very talented female forgers over the years. Look, this might help. Let me give you a brief history lesson on counterfeiting. Richard, please put the relevant photographs on the screen as I go through all this.”

“Yes boss,” replied Richard, who once again leaned forward over his two laptops. Stephen then began his talk on counterfeiting and forgers.

“Any idiot can steal,” said Stephen. “It doesn’t take much thought. Kids do it all the time in sweet shops, and if they’re not stopped they frequently end up robbing banks at gun point. Counterfeiting, on the other hand, requires both panache and finesse. Pilfering goods and services from an unwitting vendor by printing and using fake currency is as much an art form as it is a crime. The world of counterfeiters is populated by criminals, most of whom have more than the average amount of derring-do in their make-up.

"In fact, the history of counterfeiting is full of close calls, jailbreaks, Nazi plots, spectacular fraud and stacks and stacks of money.

"It used to be much easier to get away with counterfeiting money than it is today. Years ago, anyone with the means to do so and the reputation to back it up could issue notes of legal tender. With various private businesses and God knows how many banks issuing their own money, it's been estimated that around 1850, over 10,000 different kinds of currency were in circulation in the United States alone. These days however, the determination of various governments to fight counterfeiting with greatly increased security measures such as highly detailed paper currency and far tighter banking restrictions, all go to make counterfeiting increasingly more difficult. As I said, it is now a dying criminal pursuit, thank God.

"One of the most prolific counterfeiting rings in the UK, and possibly in the world, was a gang led by Stephen Jory and Kenneth Mainstone, and the gang came to be known as the modern day 'Lavender Hill Mob'."

"I've heard of them," said Sam. "Wasn't there a film made about them?"

"Yes, there was a film called 'The Lavender Hill Mob', but that starred people like Sir Alec Guiness and Stanley Holloway. It was a comedy film from Ealing Studios, but I'm afraid it wasn't about this intrepid bunch."

Richard put a photograph of the modern day 'Lavender Hill Mob' on the screen.

"Now Stephen Jory," continued Stephen, "was described as an 'old-school rogue' and Kenneth Mainstone was a retired printer. In the early 1990s, Jory and Mainstone got together with several other underworld types and began printing fake pound notes, which eventually totaled around fifty million pounds. The gang came under scrutiny after an accomplice had a small run-in with the police. It's reasonable to assume that they would've attracted attention anyway as Jory was already a well-known counterfeiter. Out of interest, he was also the guy credited with pioneering the knock-off perfume market. However, despite their undoubted skill, Scotland Yard eventually took the entire gang down one by one in a sting known as Operation Mermaid. Jory and three other members confessed, and Jory received an eight-year prison sentence. Mainstone and another accomplice stood trial and were also convicted. As a result of their exploits, the Bank of England decided to change the design of its twenty-pound note to include far more security features. Incidentally, Stephen Jory wrote several books about his criminal past, including one which became a bestseller entitled 'Funny Money'. It was quite a good read actually, and I got him to autograph my copy. Jory died in 2006."

"You mentioned 'Nazi plots' in your introduction Stephen," I said. "What on earth had they to do with counterfeiting?'

"Well apart from the genocide of the Jews, Catholics, homosexuals and many other groups, the Nazis also spent a lot of World War Two counterfeiting currency. An SS officer named Bernhard Kruger was put in charge, and he used concentration camp inmates with printing skills in a secret camp at Sachsenhausen, which is near Oranienburg in Germany, about a hundred miles North of Berlin, I think. He had them working all day and all night producing counterfeit British pound notes and US dollars. The Nazis produced over five hundred million pounds in counterfeit one and five-pound notes, equal to about five billion pounds in today's money."

"What the hell was there to buy for five billion pounds back in the 1940s and in the middle of a world war?" asked Kurt.

"The Nazis weren't in the least bit interested in buying anything," replied Stephen.

"Their sole purpose, and the motive behind Operation Bernhard, as it was called, was to introduce enough fake money into Britain to destroy its economy with a sudden influx of cash. The Nazi's had similar plans for the American economy, but the Soviets invaded Berlin soon after the forced laborers at Sachsenhausen had mastered the counterfeit hundred-dollar bill. In reality, the Nazis were brilliant counterfeiters, and were never actually caught at counterfeiting. They just lost the war."

“How come we’ve never heard about this before?” asked Helena.

“Well I’m sure it would have been mentioned at some point during your history lessons in school Helena,” replied Stephen. “But to be frank children don’t pay much attention to economic warfare at that age, particularly when there are far more juicy subjects such as torture and mass murder to concentrate on. I’m not making a point other than kids are kids the world over, and most schoolboys love guns and fighting, not economics. Girls usually don’t want to know about war and consequently tend to switch off whenever the subject arises.”

“Please carry on with your history lesson on counterfeiters Stephen,” requested Sam. “I’m finding it really interesting.”

“OK. In that case let’s go back to the 1860s and look briefly at one Charles Ulrich.”

Again, Richard put the relevant photograph onto the large TV screen.

“Ulrich was an American who had as much of a flair for attracting women as he had for creating flawless plates for printing counterfeit hundred-dollar bills. In the 1860s, the young Ulrich made a name for himself in New York as a gifted engraver of plates used for counterfeiting hundred-dollar bills. By the time he finally gave up his life of crime and confessed during his trial in 1868, Ulrich estimated that he’d produced phony bills equal to nearly $1.3 million in today’s money.”

“I’ve never heard about any of these people,” said an amazed-looking Sam.

“Well I’m sure you are all familiar with the story of Frank Abagnale. His life was made into a very successful feature film starring Leonardo DiCaprio as Abagnale and Tom Hanks as the FBI guy who eventually caught him. I won’t bother to go over all the details here, but if you want a really good insight into the mind of a top-quality counterfeiter, watch the film again. Now coming back to more modern times, let me introduce our first female,” continued Stephen.

“The wonderful story of Miss Amy Blackstone. Amy was born an only child and was brought up in Bristol by her father, a retired banker who doted on her after his wife died of cancer. Amy made her counterfeit plates in a small art studio bought and paid for by her father, which overlooked the Clifton Suspension

Bridge. Her father also gave her a very generous monthly allowance. Amy had a flair for art, and having sailed through both her GCSEs and A levels, she was offered a place at the Slade School of Art where she learnt numerous new skills, one of which was the art of the engraver. After leaving Art College, she decided the life of an impoverished artist wasn't for her, and she wasn't the least bit interested in teaching, so she used her time and her father's allowance to develop her skills in forging UK and European currency. She concentrated initially on making counterfeit plates for both British fifty-pound notes and European fifty-euro notes.

After several years, she felt her skills were good enough to start touting around the underworld, and she eventually teamed up with a guy named Peter Gardner, who also became her lover. Peter was a successful small time thief, but his main redeeming feature, apart from his good looks, was that he'd never been caught, and although the police were aware of him they had no evidence against him."

"We're back to the no evidence situation," said Paul. "It's vital in everything we do."

"Amy and Peter enlisted the help of a team of ten men and women whose job was to launder their counterfeit money around the country and in Europe. They spread out, concentrating on London, Birmingham and Manchester in the UK, and Germany and France in Europe. They had very successfully shifted over three million pounds worth of counterfeit when one of the team, Duncan McCormack, a Scotsman working for them in Munich, had had too much to drink and he made a tactless comment about the Nazis in a bar in Marienplatz. The bar happened to be full of modern day right wing neo-Nazis, and they took exception to his comments and beat him to a pulp. The police arrived, arrested everyone in sight, and in the process found over two hundred thousand euros in Duncan's briefcase. To cut a long story short, having carefully examined the money they realized it was top quality counterfeit, sweated him until he spilled his guts and told the German police about the forgeries, and in particular about Amy and Peter. The German police informed the British police, and Amy's counterfeiting days were over. She is currently serving eight years, but with parole she should be out in about three months."

“Please bear in mind,” said Paul. “Amy Blackstone was not caught because her product was bad. It was in fact brilliant, top quality counterfeit. She got caught because a drunken Scotsman in Munich couldn’t keep his opinions to himself. It’s funny how it’s the little things that eventually lead to a conviction.”

Stephen continued,

“Look, I won’t keep going on about the history of counterfeiters, I think you’ve all got the picture by now. But what I will say is this. Nine times out of ten, top counterfeiters have a brilliant brain to go with their undoubted artistic skills, and as we’ve just seen, it’s not just men that make excellent counterfeiters and forgers. So no, I’m not ruling out the possibility that the number one counterfeiter in the world may be female.”

Chapter Five

"So, what do we know about this number one?" asked Kurt. "And as much as we love you Stephen, why have you asked Helena and me to be here?"

"If you remember Kurt, I said there were five things that we can safely assume about our number one. To recap, they are as follows: One, he or she has a team of at least ten full time criminals working on this. Two, we believe they've taken on at least sixty or seventy grunts to do their spade work. Three, in order to have this much counterfeit cash to shift, they must have a very large and extremely efficient printing facility somewhere. Four, having seen the quality of the counterfeit they're producing, they must have an absolutely brilliant forger on their books to make the printing plates, and Five, we believe there are only five master counterfeiters in the world capable of doing such top quality work. We know exactly where four of them are, and we don't believe our forger is UK based. Hence we would like to see Interpol involved."

"Can you put any detail on some of your points Stephen?" asked Helena.

"Of course," replied Stephen. "Although Paul can probably explain it better as he has been doing most of the background investigation work."

"Basically," began Paul, "we've asked Interpol to get involved because the end product of the counterfeiter's handiwork has cropped up all over Europe. There've been incidents in France, Germany, Spain, Portugal, the Netherlands and Italy, and well as here in the UK."

"How do you know this is all the work of the same counterfeiter?" asked Helena. "Surely there are other counterfeiters spreading their dud notes around Europe?'

"Yes, there are," Stephen replied, "but you can easily tell the differences between the lousy forgers and our man, or woman, and I fear it's not just Europe. If their product is any good, and we know that it is in fact excellent, then they'll pretty soon be turning out counterfeit US dollars as well as euros and British pounds."

"OK," said Kurt. "If they are as you say spreading their counterfeit euros around half a dozen European countries as well as the UK, then Interpol should obviously be involved."

Kurt paused, stopped speaking and at the same time held his index figure in the air to stop anyone else speaking. He looked at the ceiling for a few seconds, and then wagging his finger in the air, he said;

"You know, something comes to mind here, Stephen. You mentioned the possibility of them spreading their wings and hitting the States. Do you remember, Helena, we received a report from Interpol in America just last week stating that someone had paid cash for a sailing boat in a place called Port Townsend in Washington State? The cash turned out to be really high quality counterfeit. I just wonder if it's the same team."

"Um," mused Helena. "It could well be."

"Consider us definitely on-board Stephen," asserted Kurt. "As of now."

"Thank you, Kurt," said Stephen. "I'm glad to have you both with us."

"Look, I'm afraid I have several other investigations going on in Europe that I have to give my attention to, and so I shall have to get back to the Netherlands," said Kurt.

"However, if Helena is happy to do so, I will ask her to take the lead on this on behalf of Interpol."

Helena nodded happily, and Kurt addressed the rest of his remarks to her.

"Excellent, in that case please make it your number one priority, clear your desk and hand everything else you're doing over to Wolfgang, your number two, and if it is OK with Stephen, can I suggest you base yourself here in Greenwich. Besides, I know how much you enjoy working with all of these folk, particularly Sam and Michael here."

"Talking of us," I said, "what's out first job?"

"You, my intrepid friends, are going to Monaco and the town of Grasse, on the Riviera in the South of France," said Paul.

"Counterfeit Euros have turned up in numerous different shops throughout both towns."

"Isn't Grasse famous for producing perfume?" asked Sam.

"It most certainly is. The French call it the perfume capital of the world."

"In that case, I'm coming as well," smiled Helena.

"My God Paul," I pleaded. "You're sending me, along with two highly extravagant women, to the perfume capital of the world. Are trying to bankrupt me?"

"Sorry mate," he replied. "We've got to follow the euros."

"Apart from buying lots of perfume," giggled Sam, "what do you want us to do?"

"I can supply you with a list of all the shops that have reported having been told by their banks that they've received counterfeit euros," said Paul. "Go to the shops and try and get descriptions of the people they think may have been passing these notes. They were mostly fifty-euro notes, and so they may well remember the customer. Then compare your lists. If you find the same description, i.e. a bald man, wearing an eye patch and a wooden leg, then he's definitely your man."

"If only it was going to be that easy," said Sam.

"Actually, you'll be amazed at how quickly descriptions come together. It may be something really small like a mole on his chin, or a beauty spot on her left cheek. You'll be amazed how people remember these small things."

"What about the language?" I asked. "My French is virtually non-existent."

"I got an A level in French," said Sam. "But I've probably forgotten most of it. Hopefully, it will come back to me," she sighed.

"It sounds like it's a good job I'm coming with you," said Helena. "I'm fluent, although I do speak with a Paris accent, and we're all heading for the south of France. I'm sure they will understand me though, even if they know I'm not a local."

"Now before you head off," said Stephen addressing me, "there are some papers you and Sam need to sign."

"What now? Don't tell me the date on Police Consultant forms we signed so we could work on the Mijas Murderer case have lapsed?"

"No," said Kurt, "they are still fine, no, these are forms I brought with me. I'm afraid being a Metropolitan Police Consultant in the South of France will mean nothing and carry no weight with French citizens. These are so that you have some authority temporarily, and I emphasize the word temporarily, appointing you both as Interpol Consultant Investigation Officers."

Kurt carefully placed two black leather wallets on the table, both of which contained printed ID on the right side, and on the left what looked like silver and gold shield shaped metal badges attached to the inside. The badges were mainly silver in color with the word 'Police' embossed in blue enamel across the top of the badge, and the words 'Consultant Investigator' also embossed in smaller blue enamel across the bottom. In big block gold-colored capital letters right across the middle, the badges simply said 'INTERPOL'. They reminded me of the badges US Marshalls used to wear in the old western films."

"Read the forms thoroughly," said Helena, "Then sign and date them. Only then can you have your badges, and remember, once you sign those forms, in theory I become your boss, only in reality I know you will both take no notice of me whatsoever."

"You know us so well," I smiled, and Helena laughed.

"Seriously though, you two," said Kurt. "Helena and I are trusting you both to behave responsibly, and not to let Interpol or us down, which I'm sure you won't. Now I have to leave, I've got a flight to catch to Amsterdam, but I'll keep in touch via Helena. Good luck to you both."

Kurt left the conference room and we spent the next half hour discussing flights and hire cars. Richard then took us through a ten-minute video presentation in what to look for in spotting counterfeit notes. After that, the three of us headed back to our hotel, had an excellent meal together in the hotel's restaurant, and the following morning we headed to Gatwick, and our flight to the French Riviera.

Chapter Six

If you've never been to the French Riviera I can thoroughly recommend it. The three of us flew into Aéroport Nice Côte d'Azur, and picked up our hire car, a silver Ford Mondeo. Helena had decided we would stay in Monaco rather than Grasse, and she had pre-booked us into the rather splendid Fairmont Hotel with two adjoining double rooms, both with sea and marina views, one for Sam and me, and one for herself. Sam and I walked through the adjoining door into Helena's room, and then the three of us sat round the table on her balcony overlooking the marina, with three glasses and a nice bottle of French Merlot we'd happily acquired at the wine shop in the foyer.

"How much do you two actually know about Monaco?" asked Helena.

"Nothing much," said Sam, "other than what I've seen on TV.'

"I do know Monaco is a playground for the ultra-rich and very famous," I said. "Mainly I suppose, due to its tax laws, which I understand are virtually non-existent."

"Spot on," said Helena. "Did you know that in 2014, thirty percent of Monaco's population was made up of millionaires? That's far more than either Zürich or Geneva. Monaco has no income tax whatsoever, low business taxes, and is well known all over the world for being a tax haven. The place is surrounded on three sides by France, with the fourth side being open to the sea, but it is very much a separate country in its own right with its own laws, one of which relates directly to money, and that is why we are here. As well as Grasse, there were numerous places here in Monaco that had been on the receiving end of our counterfeiter's dodgy fifty, one hundred and five hundred-euro notes, and Monte Carlo, the ultra-wealthy area of Monaco, was targeted."

The Marina in the Principality of Monaco

Monaco's world famous casino is the domed building in the centre of the photograph

"Didn't Grace Kelly marry the King after she'd made a film here?" asked Sam.

"Yes, that was Prince Rainier the third," replied Helena. "And when she married, she became Princess of Monaco. I bet you didn't know that when she married her prince, she acquired 142 official titles, each of which was recited in full during the wedding ceremony. The film she was making when they first met was Alfred Hitchcock's 'To Catch a Thief' with Cary Grant, who became a lifelong friend, and then while making her last ever film, the musical 'High Society' with Bing Crosby, Frank Sinatra, and Louis Armstrong, she wore her own engagement ring, the one Prince Rainier had given her, rather than a studio prop."

"Wow, how come you know so much about Grace Kelly?" Sam asked her.

"Oh, I just love all the films of that era, and I've got all of them on DVD box sets back in my apartment. Now come on, let's get back to business."

"So, is there still a prince in charge now?" asked Sam.

"Yes, there is," replied Helena. "Monaco is what's called a principality. It's governed under a form of constitutional monarchy, and currently Prince Albert II, who is Prince Rainier and Grace Kelly's only son, is the head of state. Although he is only a constitutional monarch, he still wields immense political power. His family, 'The House of Grimaldi' has ruled Monaco, with only a couple of brief interruptions, since 1297. Monaco's sovereignty was officially recognized by the Franco-Monegasque Treaty in 1861, and Monaco became a full voting member of the United Nations in 1993."

"Just how big is Monaco?" I asked.

"It's incredibly small actually," replied Helena. "Monaco has a land area of just two square kilometers, making it the second smallest country in the world after the Vatican City, which only covers half a square kilometer. However, Monaco has a population of just over thirty eight thousand, and that means with nineteen thousand inhabitants per square kilometer, Monaco also happens to be the most densely populated country in the world."

"Is Monaco in the EU?" asked Sam

"Good question," replied Helena. "The principality is not formally a part of the European Union, but it participates in certain EU policies, including customs and border controls. Monaco joined the Council of Europe in 2004, and through its close relationship with France, Monaco now uses the euro as its sole currency."

"Bringing us back to the reason we are here." I said.

"Exactly," stated Helena.

"But why are we starting here rather than Grasse?" asked Sam. "Not that I'm complaining. The view across the marina from this balcony is absolutely amazing."

"The reason is simple – cooperation. We need to get information, and that means getting as many highly detailed descriptions as possible, and the good citizens of Monaco are far more likely to be helpful than the average Frenchmen. To be honest, I hold out little hope of getting decent descriptions from any of the shopkeepers in Grasse. They are like most other French people in that they don't willingly cooperate with Interpol, or the French police for that matter, but because of the international make-up of the people of Monaco, I think they'll be more willing to help."

"What's the French beef with Interpol and the police?" I asked.

"Nothing in particular," replied Helena. "They just don't like authority figures, in any shape or form. In most things, the French give the impression that the rest of us are not worth bothering with. They all seem to have this superior opinion of themselves, which I think stems from both the Napoleonic era and the De Gaulle era. They both continually told the French that they were so much better than any other nations. Their food was better, their wine was better, their scenery was better, their music, art and culture were better and if the world had had any sense of honor, the international language of the world would be French and not English."

After breakfast the following morning, Helena split up the list of Monaco retail premises that had received counterfeit euros into three piles, one each.

"Our task today is very simple. We've been given these lists by four different banks in Monaco. These are the various retailers and businesses that have been on the receiving end of dud money. Our job this morning is simply to go and see the shopkeepers, managers etc. on the list, and see if they can remember what the person that paid them looked like. Man, or woman, black or white, what sort of age, glasses, beards or moustaches, any scars, beauty spots, literally anything they can remember. Now in most cases, they paid for whatever they bought with numerous fifty, hundred or five hundred-euro notes, and most places should remember that. Write everything down and let's meet up back here at midday and see what we've got, if anything."

"Any recommended procedure?" asked Sam.

"Start by showing whoever you're talking to your Interpol badges, that gives you authority, and then tell them that you're making enquiries that may hopefully result in the return of their goods. That should encourage them to be as helpful to you as much as they can, but please make no promises."

"Anything else?" I asked Helena.

"No, just use your common sense. See you back here at midday for coffee."

We split up and headed off on foot in three different directions. The first premises on my list was a marine equipment retailers where our crooks had bought a pair of 100cc outboard boat engines for €18,000, paying with thirty-six counterfeit five-hundred euro notes. The shop was empty of customers, but there were two men behind the counter, an older man in his fifties and a lad of about eighteen or nineteen, I estimated. I started by showing them my Interpol badge and asking if the older of the two men in front of me spoke English.

"Yes, I speak English," he replied in a strong French accent.

"Good morning, sir," I began, "I'm looking for the manager, Mr. Antoine Colbert."

"That is me," he replied. I shook his hand and continued.

"I'm making enquiries about the counterfeit one-hundred and five-hundred euro notes that were recently passed around Monaco. I gather you received thirty-six of the five-hundred euro notes in exchange for two brand new Yamaha 100cc outboard engines."

"I did, and please tell me you've come to let me know you've got my engines back?"

"No, I'm afraid not at this stage, sir, but we are following up several good leads, and it would help us very much if you could give us a good description of whoever you sold the engines to. As much detail as you can remember."

"Well, I think he was like you – English," replied Monsieur Colbert. "He spoke passable French, but with an English accent. He was tall, around one hundred and eighty centimeters, or roughly six feet as you English still insist on using. He had fairly tidy short blonde hair, and he wore steel framed blue tinted sunglasses, even inside the shop, although I thought nothing of it at the time."

"Great," I responded. "Any beard, moustache, scars, anything else you can remember about him. How was he dressed for example?"

"No, no scars or facial hair. He wore a dark blue tee shirt and white trousers, Oh, and he had a bright red cap with him, but he was carrying it, not wearing it."

"A baseball cap?" I asked.

"No, a standard boating style cap, but bright red, not the usual blue or white."

"Did the tee shirt have any logos on it?"

"No, it was just plain dark blue."

"So how did he take the engines away, sir?"

"He had a big white van parked outside, and we simply put them in the back."

"Did the van have any logos on it?"

"No, I'm pretty sure it was a hired van as it had a Hertz sticker on the windscreen."

"Did the fact he paid in cash seem unusual to you, and did you ask him about it?"

"I didn't need to ask. He told me he'd had a really good win the night before in the Monte Carlo Casino, and that he'd decided to blow it on a pair of new outboard engines for his boat before his wife spent it all on designer handbags and new shoes. In fact, we both laughed about it, although I'm not laughing so much now."

"No, I can imagine. Well I can't think of anything else at this stage Monsieur Colbert. Thank you so much for all your help, and we'll be in touch if we have any news for you."

"Yes, well I won't be holding my breath as you English say."

And on that cheerful note, I left the shop.

During the rest of the morning I visited another eleven shops. Some could remember the purchaser quite well, others not quite so well, and three couldn't even remember whether it had been a man or a woman that had passed the notes. Just before midday the three of us met up again, congregated in the pleasant lounge area of the hotel and compared notes over some strong French coffee.

"So, how have we got on?" asked Helena.

"Well I've visited nine retailers and got five good descriptions," said Sam.

"I've done eleven retailers and got six good descriptions," I countered.

"I win," smiled Helena. "Fourteen shops and nine good descriptions."

"I think you said the winner had to pay for the meal tonight," I said, smiling as I glanced over at Sam, who immediately responded.

"Yes, I distinctly remember you saying that as well Helena."

"Yes, well it doesn't matter which one of us pays as Interpol will be picking up the tab anyway, you pair of crooks," she laughed and then continued.

"So, any conclusions to be drawn from this morning's interviews. Sam?" Helena asked.

"Well if I had to draw a conclusion I would say there was a team of two passing the notes round Monaco. Both English, one man and one woman. I've received fairly similar descriptions from all those that could remember where the counterfeit came from, and the descriptions lead me to think there were just the two of them."

"That coincides exactly with my thoughts," I said. "I got three pretty good descriptions of the man, about six feet tall, with short blond hair, and the woman was also blonde, but shoulder length hair and around five feet six or seven. Both of them by the sound of it were in their mid-thirties. I had no descriptions of anyone else that would introduce a third person, nobody other than these two. Incidentally, the young lad at the boat yard said the van they were using was definitely a long wheel base white Ford Transit hired from Hertz. Apparently, he noticed it because he's a bit of a petrol head."

"I'm sorry, what is a 'petrol head'?" asked Helena.

"Oh, sorry Helena, it means someone who is really into cars." I replied.

"I see. Well anyway, it was much the same with me," said Helena. "Several people gave me good descriptions, and all of them agree with yours. So, if that's the case, I think we've done as much as we can here and we might as well drive up to Grasse and do the same exercise there this afternoon. I suspect we'll find the same two descriptions coming from there as I now suspect this pair were sent to the South of France, where it sounds like they hired a long wheel base Ford Transit from Hertz, then drove round to various different types of high end retailers buying up expensive equipment they could then easily sell on. I'm also assuming they left Monaco later that same day, as all the purchases were made on the same day, and if I was them I'd want to be out of there long before the banks spotted the fakes."

"Being English, do you think that means the gang is based in England?" asked Sam.

"No, I don't think so," replied Helena. "As Stephen said before we left, we've been referring to the counterfeiter as the 'Faro Forger' all along, although we don't know exactly where in the Algarve he's based. It's just that what little we do know all seems to indicate the counterfeit cash is being printed somewhere in the Algarve, and the name, the 'Faro Forger' sounded good."

"So, do you think the counterfeiter is Portuguese?' I asked.

"To be honest Michael, we haven't a clue. He could be a disillusioned Tibetan monk, a Zulu warrior who hates the civilized world, a Norwegian sailor who's saving up to buy his own fleet of cruise ships or the Albanian Ambassador to Mongolia who is looking for something more interesting in his life. We know his work, or should I say their work as it still may be a woman, but we know nothing about the actual counterfeiter. Come on, let's finish our coffee, drive up to Grasse, and do the rounds up there after lunch. If, as we suspect, it confirms our suspicions of an English man and woman team hitting the south of France, we'll come back here, have a decent meal on Interpol tonight, get some sleep and then fly back to London in the morning."

If you've never been there, Grasse is well worth a visit. They call themselves the perfume capital of the world, and it is impossible to get away from perfume. The town is not what you'd call massive, but it has a great location, being perched on the top of a hill with magnificent views. There are countless small streets, every one of which is littered with perfume shops of varying sizes selling 'souvenir' perfumes costing very little, to really smart retail outlets selling highly specialist perfumes costing thousands of euros an ounce. You can even buy custom made perfumes designed to your own specifications, plus all the necessary paraphernalia that goes with perfume: bottles, jars, sprayers, aerosols etc. etc.

As I said, top of the range exclusive perfume can get extremely expensive, and just to prove my point I was informed during my visits to various perfume shops and museums in Grasse about the perfume that holds the World Record title as the most expensive perfume in the world. It was released in 2005, with only ten bottles available of this super-rare, super-exclusive, limited-edition perfume. It was released for sale in both Harrods store in London and Bergdorf Goodman in New York. The 'No. 1 Imperial Majesty' as it was branded, in reality was just a Clive Christian No. 1, in a very fancy bottle. Each bottle contained just 16.9 ounces of perfume, for which the cost for a bottle was $215,000. Crazy!

We did the rounds of Grasse just as we had in Monaco, and pretty soon came to exactly the same conclusions. The South of France had been hit by a male and female two-man team. They'd easily shifted hundreds of thousands of euros during the day, mainly buying top of the range perfumes, and then left with their contraband loaded in the back of their white Ford Transit the same day they'd arrived. We suspected they had either unloaded all their ill-gotten gains straight onto a ship in the docks or stored it all in a warehouse somewhere for later collection and onward sale. They then must have returned the van to Hertz so as not to raise any suspicions. Finding out exactly who hired the van though might be helpful.

At Helena's suggestion, I tried ringing several Hertz car hire depots in the south of France, and I eventually found the one I wanted in Cannes. They told me our couple had in fact hired two long wheel base transit vans on the days in question, both white in color, and they were described by the lady at Hertz as "A lovely couple who were moving to the area from Marseilles with their two sons." I asked her if she had seen the two boys as well, but apparently they were both still at their boarding school in Switzerland. She did however have the couple's passport and driving license details on file, and she said she would email a copy to me at our hotel. We knew the names would obviously be false, the passports would be false and the driving licenses would be false, but the one thing that had to be true were the photographs on the documents. The email arrived later, and we now had two decent quality color photographs taken from their false passports. I recognized the blond man immediately. It was the bastard that had skimmed my Amex card in Greenwich. The highly elusive Mr. Donald Preston.

We all agreed, our couple was now long gone; there being little point in our staying, after an evening meal and a good night's rest we flew back to London on the early flight.

Chapter Seven

"I trust you three have got plenty of clean clothes?" said Stephen. "Kurt's been on the phone while you've been sunning yourselves on the French Riviera, and he's convinced the counterfeit currency found in the States is produced by the same team. He suggests you three head off to Port Townsend as soon as you can."

"Thanks for the welcome back Stephen," I said smiling at him. "I missed you too."

"What do you want from me Michael, a slap on the back, a shake of the hand or a big sloppy kiss?" demanded Stephen, obviously not in a good mood.

"My, my," said Sam very soothingly. "We are Mr. Grumpy today, aren't we?"

"Oh, sorry guys," said Stephen. "As you may have guessed, I'm not having a good day. Sit yourselves down and I'll order some tea. Paul's giving evidence in court, but he should be back any minute. You know sometimes this job drives me mad. I get so frustrated with working all the hours God sends, never seeing my wife and kids in daylight, and seemingly getting nowhere due to bent solicitors sticking up for the bloody crooks."

"But even the worst crooks are entitled to be defended," said Sam.

"Well they shouldn't be," said Stephen in a grumpy voice, and then he laughed.

"Well we think we've actually got somewhere," I replied. "We've got reasonably decent color photographs of the two operatives that worked the south of France."

"Oh, well done you three. Great news," said Stephen, looking at us all. I showed him the photographs and he immediately picked up his phone, dialed an extension and asked Richard to come to his office, complete with laptop. Richard duly arrived with his laptop, and also with Paul in tow who had just returned from court.

"Hi all," Paul said, kissing both Sam and Helena on their cheeks and shaking my hand. He then turned to Stephen and exclaimed, "Matheson and Protheroe were found guilty, Stephen. Unanimous verdicts and the judge gave the little creeps twelve years."

"Well, that's a lot better than we thought," said Stephen. "Perhaps, this is going to be a good day after all. These guys have also done well and come back from the south of France with photos of the two that have been working the area."

Richard having connected his laptop to the police station's internal network and also having scanned the two photographs, projected their faces on to the screen.

"That's the rotten little sod I tried to arrest at the hotel down the road, but he'd done a runner before I got there," exclaimed Paul.

"Yup," I said. "I can also confirm that he's the guy that skimmed my card. I've no idea who the woman is though."

"You mentioned Kurt," said Helena. "Do I need to phone him?"

"No, don't worry Helena, he'll now be in his meeting with the German Federal Minister of Justice and Consumer Protection which he thinks is probably going to last for hours, so if it's OK with you he asked me if I'd brief you?"

"OK, that's fine by me," said Helena.

"So, Port Townsend," said Sam. "Where the hell is that? To be honest Stephen, until Kurt mentioned it in the meeting I'd never heard of it. What about you Michael?"

As Sam asked the question, Richard put a map of Washington State on the big screen.

"Likewise," I replied. "But I did Google it. Apparently, its main claim to fame is that it's where they filmed 'An Officer and a Gentleman' with Richard Gere and Debra Winger."

"Ooh," said Helena. "That's the one where he's dressed in that gorgeous white Navy uniform, sweeps the girl her off her feet and carries her out through the timber factory."

"Yeah, that's the one," I said.

"Anyway, as you can see," I continued, using Stephen's red laser torch to point at the screen,

"Port Townsend is located here, right at the top of Puget Sound, overlooking the US Navy's only entrance to its naval base at Bremerton. The nearest airport looks like being Seattle."

"It is," said Stephen

"And both British Airways and Virgin fly there every day from London, but I haven't booked anything as I didn't know how soon you wanted to leave."

"What details do we know, and from whom, about how the counterfeit notes turned up in Port Townsend?" asked Helena.

"It was Interpol in the United States," answered Paul, "that issued a general round robin memo to all countries saying forged currency had turned up in Port Townsend. Most people refer to the place as PT for short I gather, so I will as well. According to the FBI, a very wealthy looking Dutch couple turned up in PT about three months ago, and then on the Wednesday morning they negotiated the purchase of a deluxe sailing boat that one of the local shipping brokers had in his shipyard. They agreed a price of four million US dollars with him, on condition the boat was in the water and ready to sail away when they returned on Friday afternoon with the necessary funds. He was expecting a bank draft, but they arrived late Friday afternoon with three suitcases full of one-hundred dollar bills."

"After the banks had closed?" I asked, sort of already knowing the answer.

"Exactly," confirmed Paul.

"Bloody hell," said Sam. "If my Math is correct, that's forty thousand one-hundred dollar bills. How the hell did they explain that?"

"Oh, they told him they'd taken the money out of one of their offshore Cayman Island accounts, and their motto was, 'If the taxman doesn't know about it, then he can't tax it'. They suggested the broker simply kept the cash in a safety deposit box at his own bank where he could put it in and take it out any time he wanted without the taxman knowing a thing about it. Being the stupid greedy fool that he was and not wanting to lose a large chunk of it in tax, he agreed. The broker took the three suitcases from the buyers and waved them goodbye as they sailed away, never to be seen again. His bank was closed over the weekend, as the counterfeiters knew, and the broker didn't get to his bank until the following Monday morning. He took out a five-year agreement with the bank on a large metal container for use with his new safety deposit box, into which he placed the contents of the two cases. He never went near the money again until last month when he decided to blow some of it on a new car for his wife's birthday. The car salesman paid the twenty-five thousand dollars in one-hundred dollar bills into his own bank in the normal way, but the bank decided to look closely at the cash as it was a large amount. It took a while, but they realized they'd got top quality counterfeit on their hands, and so they contacted the FBI who after some initial investigation eventually realized it was an international crime, and so reluctantly they contacted Interpol. Interpol in the States contacted Interpol Europe, and here we are."

"Wow!" exclaimed Sam. "So, what do you want us to do Helena?" she asked.

"I think we need to go to PT," she replied, "and see if we can find out exactly where our four-million-dollar yacht disappeared to.

Chapter Eight

You'd think it would be easy, wouldn't you? Just jump on a plane to Seattle airport, hire a car, and drive to your destination, but having looked at our options, we couldn't decide which one to take. Whatever we did, we had to fly to Seattle first, but then it was either an hour's ride in a small plane, a three-hour drive South round the bottom of Puget Sound and then up the other side, or we could drive the straighter and more direct route, but that entailed island hopping using numerous ferries.

"OK?" I said.

"Helena, what are we going to do when we get there? Once we know that it might make our decision easier."

"Well surely we look for our missing boat?" said Sam.

"Yes, agreed," said Helena, but we know it's not in Port Townsend anymore, so we have to visit other ports and harbors and see if we can spot it."

"But you can see from the map of the area, the place is awash with islands?" queried Sam.

"Our missing boat could be hiding in any one of them, and I bet there aren't ferries going to all the small islands."

"The answer's simple then, isn't it?" I queried. "Don't hire a car, hire a boat. It's the only way we can look around all these small islands. Plus, the fact our boat thieves might have gone North and be hiding in the islands, they might have gone even further north towards Victoria and sailed into Canadian waters, or they may have turned left…"

"I think you mean turned to port dear," corrected a smiling Sam.

"Thank you, my dearest," I replied as both Stephen and Paul sniggered.

"So, as I was saying," I said pointing at the map, "they might have turned to port, gone out of the straits of Juan de Fuca and then headed south for any of the harbors down the Pacific coast.

We need to be able to search them all. Alternatively, how about using a light aircraft that can swoop down if we see a boat matching the description of our missing boat."

"Hold your fire, Biggles," said Stephen.

"I am sorry," said Helena. "Who or what is Biggles? It is a term I am not familiar with."

"Sorry Helena," replied Stephen.

"Biggles was a fictional British pilot in World War One who was the best pilot the world had ever known, at least according to his creator."

"Oh, I see," said Helena. "But I do see what Stephen is getting at. We want to find the boat without the people who stole it knowing we've found it, and we can't really do that by swooping down on them like a kamikaze pilot."

"Biggles wasn't a kamikaze pilot," I protested. "They were Japanese suicide pilots who flew in World War Two."

"Does it matter Michael?" asked Sam.

"Well I'm sure it would matter to Biggles," I said in my best sulky voice.

"Look," said Stephen. "Can I make a suggestion? Fly to Seattle and I'll arrange to have a suitable boat waiting for you somewhere in the area. If it's a decent boat then you can travel just as fast as you will be steering in straight lines for the most part instead of having to follow small roads in a car."

"I wouldn't have a clue about what sort of boat you'd need to hire," I said. "I've steered a cabin cruiser on the Norfolk Broads, but that's about it."

The two girls also confirmed that they knew nothing about boats either.

"Well in that case leave it to me?" asked Stephen. "As it happens I love deep sea fishing and I go out whenever I can, especially in American waters, and over the years I've learnt quite a lot through talking to the various captains. I'll have a good look around on the internet, see what's available, and I assume Helena I can charge the charter to the Interpol private citizen's charge card?"

"Of course, Stephen, and thank you. That would be incredibly helpful."

"If you don't mind me asking?" queried Sam. "What on earth is the Interpol private citizen's charge card?"

"Oh, that's all right," said Helena. "It's a special Visa charge card with no upper limit. Interpol guarantees and pays all bills without question, but it's all done in the name of two private citizens so that nobody knows Interpol is involved. Stephen, I have a favor to ask."

"Yeees," said Stephen very slowly.

"On this trip we are going to need someone highly technical who can track any boat using small magnetic tracking devices, operate a drone if needed and blend in with the three of us. Sam and Michael are obviously a couple, but I'll need to have a fake husband for this trip. Obviously, Richard would be the ideal person to take with us, if he is willing. Any chance Interpol can borrow him on secondment for a month or so?"

We all looked at Richard who was now smiling from ear to ear and vigorously nodding his head. We then all looked at Stephen who was looking very non-committal.

"Answer me honestly Richard," began Stephen. "Can the rest of your team manage without you for a month or more if necessary? Think carefully before you answer, because if you say yes I may decide you're not needed at all and save the department some money."

"They are all extremely well trained," began Richard. "And yes, they can manage without me for a short period of time, but in the long run, I'm still needed to oversee and keep on top of everything and ensure all new developments are studied and introduced."

"Nicely done Richard," smiled Sam.

"You do realize," I said, "that if we get into a sticky situation Richard, you may have to kiss Helena in order to convince people you're married. Bearing that in mind, are you really sure you want to come with us."

Richard had now gone bright red, and he looked sheepishly at Helena.

"Ignore him, Richard," said Helena smiling. "I shall look forward to our first kiss as husband and wife should the need arise."

"If there's going to be lots of kissing, can I come instead?" asked Paul.

"You don't have the necessary skills, Paul," said Helena.

We all laughed and then we all looked at Stephen for an answer.

"Yes, of course you can go Richard. This is important and we need to give Interpol whatever support they need. Just make sure you come back in one piece. I'll charter a suitable boat for you, and in the meantime Richard can get together a complete list of whatever technical bits and pieces you need and will be using. Anything that doesn't come back with you I'll charge to Interpol."

"No problem," said Helena. "And Stephen, many thanks for your help."

Chapter Nine

Two days later the four of us flew British Airways to Seattle/Tacoma, all of us travelling as private citizens. All Richard's equipment and all our Interpol IDs, credit cards etc. were sent ahead by Paul in a sealed metal container marked for collection by me, that couldn't be opened or X-rayed by US customs. US police and other American agencies have a similar arrangement with the British authorities. The reason was simple, Helena didn't want the US Authorities knowing that Europe's Interpol were carrying out an investigation on their territory without being invited. Having cleared US customs and collected all our luggage, including Richard's container of goodies, we got a taxi South to Tacoma, where Stephen had a very nice motor yacht waiting for us. The boat in question was a white 59 feet long Carver Voyager Motor Yacht with twin Volvo D12-675 horse power engines. More than enough speed to catch any missing sailing boat. Inside the boat was all white fiberglass, white leather and rosewood cabinets, and the pilot house as it was officially called, or the upstairs outside bridge as I called it, was again all white leather and white fiberglass. There were three state rooms, (posh for cabins), and Sam and I shared the largest with Helena and Richard having a slightly smaller cabin each. This was the sort of yacht you would pay a small fortune to hire, I'm sorry, charter! The boating fraternity it seems have a high-falutin language all of their own.

The Hired Motor Yacht

Yacht Repairers in Port Townsend

Port Townsend on Puget Sound, Washington State

Nanaimo, Vancouver Island, British Columbia

After stowing everything (unpacking to you and me), we cast off (started the engine, untied the ropes and started moving) and headed north. We'd decided we'd take a look round the islands in Puget Sound, then continue north out of the sound and then cross into Canadian waters, in order to have a good look around the various harbors and marinas along the eastern coast of Vancouver Island. The weather was warm and sunny and all four of us were on the open top deck. I was steering. The two girls had changed into their bikinis and Richard and I were both in swimming shorts. The girls and Richard were sitting round the table on the outside deck following our route on a large detailed map, one of many that had come with the boat.

"Helena, can you please explain to me again your thinking and the reason we'll be searching Vancouver Island?" asked Sam.

"Yes, of course," replied Helena. "Although strictly speaking, it was Michael's idea, and having heard him out, I agreed with him."

"Sorry Michael, I keep forgetting you've got a brain as well as your looks," said Sam in her best sarcastic voice. I looked around the yacht's open lounge for something to throw at her but couldn't find anything suitable. At home, we leave old and unwanted paperbacks lying around the house specifically for that purpose.

"If I may continue, please ladies and gentlemen," said Helena, sounding just like my old headmistress.

"Michael's thinking was that if he'd stolen the yacht, the first thing he'd want to do was either hide it or camouflage it. Hiding it will be extremely difficult as the yacht's name 'Princess Sophie' is plastered all over the back of it in large letters, and we also know the numbers and letters printed on the sails – USP23."

"Does that mean the sail markings are all registered in a central record base somewhere?" asked Richard.

"Sadly not," I replied. "I researched that while Helena was busy doing other things. Sail numbers are issued by the boat's manufacturers, in this case US meaning it was made in America, P is for its Portland shipyard, and 23 meaning it was the 23rd yacht of this class to come off the production line. In reality, they mean nothing to anyone other than the boat's manufacturer, and therefore they're not in some central registry."

"So," continued Helena, "hiding it will be extremely difficult for several reasons. Firstly, it is over twice the length of this yacht at 120 feet, secondly its masts are very tall and they are both non-collapsible. I was reliably informed by Stephen, who seems to know all about boaty things, that the length of most yacht masts are based on a ratio of roughly 1.00 to 1.45 of the boats overall length. So at 120 feet in length, the masts of the yacht we're looking for must be roughly 175 feet high. That will be extremely hard to hide."

"If it was me," I said, "I'd try to camouflage it as soon as possible. Surely, the three main things that give any boat or yacht away are the name on the stern, the numbers on the sail, and the color of the hull."

"I agree with Michael," said Helena.

"And I think because of that we're looking for a large shipyard with either a good size dry dock, or at the very least a large support area so that the hull can be resprayed another color, the ship's name can be changed and new sails fitted. I also agree with Michael's earlier point, in that I'd want the yacht out of US waters as soon as possible, and the easiest way of doing that is to go due north up Puget Sound, and then head for the numerous coastal ports up the eastern coast of Vancouver Island, which is in Canadian waters."

"I'm also thinking," I said, "that if this was my operation the procedure would be to buy a boat with counterfeit, move it away from the scene of the crime as soon as possible, and then sell it on for real money to some poor unsuspecting soul."

"Which is basically what is happening in the top of the range car market," said Sam. "Buy a new Ferrari with dodgy money, respray the car and change the plates, and then sell it on in another country."

"Exactly," I agreed. "Except flashy yachts are worth a lot more than flashy cars."

"What do you want me to do with the technology I've brought along?" asked Richard.

"I want you husband dearest," smiled Helena, "to try and put a tracking bug on the yacht should we find it, and also on the car of whoever tips up to collect the money from the buyer, assuming the sale hasn't already gone through and the money changed hands."

"They can't own the boating equivalent of chop shops all over the place," said Sam. "They surely have to use somewhere local to where the theft takes place."

"I don't know," I replied. "But I would imagine it's just the same in the boat market as the car market. There's always a garage that will do a quick respray and plate change for some decent 'no questions asked' under the counter cash in a brown paper bag. I'm sure it's just the same with boatyards. There are good and bad guys in every business, whatever it happens to be."

"If it was me running this scam," said Richard.

"Yeees," we all said slowly and in unison.

"I'd be operating mainly in the Med. There are thousands of luxury yachts to buy with counterfeit euros, and thousands of harbors and marinas to hide them in. I think that's where I'd do the bulk of my business."

"You know, Richard's right." Sam said. "Maybe that's why the guy in Monte Carlo was buying outboard engines. They may have been for a boat conversion."

"You see," said Helena. "My husband is not just a pretty face."

Richard went bright red, yet again.

Chapter Ten

We sailed, (I use the term loosely as I don't do string and flappy bits, and my idea of boating is sun bathing on a floating gin palace with a big powerful engine, and a crew to do all the work.) Anyway, I digress – as I started to say, we sailed north checking out every bay, harbor and marina we came across in the islands north of Seattle.

This included Vashon Island, Bainbridge Island and the quite long Whidbey Island, which we were in the process of passing on our right. We took a small diversion into the lengthy bay of Marrowstone Island, but sadly there was no sign of any large yachts, and as we were emerging again back into Puget Sound we saw Port Townsend come into view on our port side. (That's on the left for any non-nautical types.)

"Why don't we stop at Port Townsend and see if the boatyard has a picture of the 'Princess Sophie' we could copy?" suggested Sam.

"Great idea," Helena replied. "I don't think I've got what you Brits call 'sea legs' and I could definitely do with standing on some hard, solid ground again."

Port Townsend describes itself in its publicity as 'One of the coolest small towns in America', and they are not referring to the weather, which was very sunny but with no humidity to speak of. We moored our own boat in the marina and went for a walk along Water Street which is the long road running virtually the entire length of the town's water frontage. We pretty soon saw what they meant. PT has several newish buildings, but the vast majority are described as being Victorian, i.e. very old in American terms. As for the buildings themselves, they are a mixture of hotels, bed and breakfast establishments, restaurants, cafes, and numerous shops selling books, antiques, objets d'art, fashion clothing etc. Everything you could possibly want to become one of the cool people, but from what I could see, not very much in the way of normal shopping. It was quite an unusual place, but nevertheless, I quite liked it.

We eventually found the boatyard that had been duped into selling the 'Princess Sophie', and Matthew Cormack, the boatyard manager, gave us a photocopy of a photograph he'd taken of the yacht just before it had been collected by our mystery couple. We told him we were doing all we could to find his boat, thanked him for his time and then headed back to our own boat. We began our search again amongst the countless small islands around the area of San Juan Island. We found lots of whales, orcas and sailing boats, but sadly not the one we were looking for.

"Let's forget around here and head straight for Victoria," I suggested.

"Is that the town at the bottom of Vancouver Island?" asked Sam.

"You make it sound as if it has sunk," joked Richard.

"Oh, it's far from sunk," I replied. "I visited there several years ago when I was doing some research for a book about Canada. I was told before I went that Victoria was very much like Great Britain. Well I tell you now, it's not. It is so much nicer. No offence to Britain or the UK, but Victoria just seems so much cleaner, fresher, and more open. I loved it."

"Get you," said Sam. "Coming over all romantic about a town."

"You wait till you see it." I said.

We changed course and an hour later headed into the harbor of Victoria. Richard, who was now at the helm (steering to you and me), slowly maneuvered our yacht around the large harbor, but we saw nothing of any interest, so we headed back out and steered due north hugging the east coast of Vancouver Island.

After several hours of searching, we decided to call it a day and give up the search until the following day. We decided to moor up for the night at the next marina we came to which as it happened turned out to be at a place named Nanaimo. As we were looking for an empty berth in which to moor up for the night, I spotted a shipyard in the far corner with several yachts under repair.

"Richard, can you ease back on the throttle a bit, and then do a gentle pass of the shipyard entrance? There are quite a few yachts with very tall masts in there, and you never know, one of them might just be the one we're looking for."

"Do shipyards always have security guards on the gate?" asked Sam. "Because that one does, although to be honest they look more like heavies than official security guards."

"You know I think we might just have found what we're searching for," I said. "Look casually at the last boat on the right. They've started sanding down the stern where the name used to be painted, but if you look carefully and squint your eyes a bit, you can just about make out the 'Pri' something or other at the beginning, and it definitely ends with something, something, 'phie'."

"Right," commanded Helena. "Everyone stop looking at the shipyard and start looking at each other. We don't want to make anyone suspicious. We're supposed to be two loving couples on holiday, so let's look like we're enjoying ourselves. Richard, I'm coming over there and you need to put your arm round my waist. Sam, can you please go and sit on Michael's lap, and nobody look at the shipyard until we're safely moored up somewhere."

"Yes boss," I replied as Sam came and plonked herself on my lap. Richard tentatively put his arm round Helena's naked waist, as both girls were still in their bikinis.

"Well that's not going to convince anyone Richard," said Helena.

"Look, do you love me or not?" she asked him. "For goodness sake man, put some effort in to it and show me, but more importantly show them how you feel." And with that Helena bent lower, put a hand either side of Richard's face, pulled it up towards her and kissed him full on the mouth. Richard didn't know quite what to do with himself or how to react, so Helena gently moved her lips and said quietly to him,

"Stop going red Richard and kiss me back for God's sake. The guards at the shipyard entrance are watching us." Richard did as he was told, and I have to say it looked to me as if he was now thoroughly enjoying the experience. As if to prove Helena's point, one of the guards wolf whistled our boat as we drifted gently past. Helena then broke away from Richard, who despite his instructions had still gone bright red, and gave the guards a completely over the top curtsy, after which the guards both gave her a round of applause.

"I thought we were trying to be discreet and go unnoticed," whispered Sam.

"We were, but that was plan A," replied Helena. "I've moved on to plan B now."

"I can't keep up," said Richard, still recovering from his amorous experience.

"Look," said Helena. "Once we're moored up, the four of us can go for a leisurely walk. You and I, Sam, should stay in our bikinis, but just put a thin silk or lacy top on, and then we'll make sure we walk past the shipyard entrance. We'll stroll along a few paces in front of the men, and I'm pretty sure the two guards will happily take time out to chat us up, while our two husbands make sure 'Princess Sophie' is where we think she is."

Sam was wearing a white bikini, which showed off her excellent tan from living in the Algarve, whereas Helena's red bikini worked really well with her paler skin, which living in Holland didn't get anywhere near the same amount of sun.

We found an empty berth, tied up and informed the marina manager, who had wandered over to talk to us, that we'd probably be just getting fuel and fresh water, but if we enjoyed the evening we may decide stay over. We took on a hell of a lot of fuel, and topped up our fresh water, and then paid him with a credit card issued by Interpol in my bogus name. The girls put on virtually see-through tops, and Richard and I both put on tee shirts and shorts. With that we locked the boat and talked over our next move as we stood on the marina.

"Do you still want me to try and put a bug on the yacht Helena?" asked Richard.

"No," she replied. "I've been thinking about that. We're not really interested in who bought it or where it goes. What we want are the people selling the yacht, and I'm not sure yet how we go about finding out who they are?" she mused.

"Perhaps we can persuade our two beefy admirers to accidently tell us while we flirt outrageously with them?" suggested Sam.

"Not too outrageous please ladies?" requested Richard.

"You're not getting jealous already are you husband dearest?" teased Helena.

"Ignore him," I said. "You girls go for it. We're not really bothered, are we Richard? After all, why should we worry about two super-tanned, muscle ridden guys with massive six packs, when you ladies have got the two of us to come back to?"

"Is that supposed to be helpful?" asked Richard, and we all laughed, including him.

"Don't worry guys," said Sam. "It's all in a good cause." And with that we headed off in the direction of the shipyard with the two girls strolling about ten paces in front of us. As the girls reached the shipyard entrance they stopped and started chatting with the two guards. The girls had walked slightly past the guards, so that in order to talk to them they had to turn their backs to Richard and me. We used this to our advantage and casually slipped into the shipyard unnoticed. I immediately wandered over and attempted to chat to the guy up the steps sanding down the back of the yacht.

"Hi," I said cheerfully.

He just looked down at me and carried on sanding.

"That looks like fairly pointless hard work to me." I continued, "Can't you just carefully paint on top of it?"

"Not if you're changing the name," he replied.

"Well, why are you changing the name?" I asked.

"I'm not," he replied. "The owners are changing it. I just do what I'm told."

"Oh," I muttered. "So, who are the owners?" I asked, trying to sound as casual as possible, and at the same time trying to keep an eye on the girls. Helena was busy feeling the biceps of one of the guards, while Sam was lightly punching the six-pack chest of the other guard.

"Some Spanish lot, I think," replied the guy up the steps. "I heard the name once and it sounded Spanish to me, but I don't speak the lingo. You'll have to ask the guys at the gate. They work for the owners and are nothing to do with us. Sorry mate."

"Oh, that's OK," I said, and wandered over to look at another boat so that I hopefully wouldn't be caught staring at the ex 'Princess Sophie' if our two guards happened to look in this direction. Glancing over, I noticed the girls still had them completely entranced, and all four of them were now laughing at something or other. I looked around, but I couldn't see Richard anywhere, so I decided to slip down between two of the yachts, and arriving at the far end of the shipyard I found Richard in the shipyard's empty office, rummaging through various papers on the desk. He clearly didn't hear me arrive, and nearly jumped out of his skin when I spoke.

"For crying out loud Richard, what the hell are you doing?" I asked him.

"Are you trying to give me a heart attack?" he asked.

"Oh, don't worry," I replied. "Helena will give you the kiss of life. I think she's taken quite a shine to you."

"No, that's just for show. Isn't it?' he asked with a sort of pleading in his voice.

"Well, do you like her or not?" I asked him.

"For goodness sake Michael, what's not to like? She's beautiful, she's sexy, she's a great kisser, she's intelligent, she speaks English and three other languages, she…"

"Yes, I get the idea. You like her. Now more importantly, did you find anything?"

"I found a letter mentioning 'Princess Sophie' so remembering your burglar's thing in the Bahamas about leaving everything as you found it, I copied it on their photocopier and then put the original back in the same place on the desk. I've got the photocopy in my pocket. Do you want to read it?"

"Yes, but not here and not now. Let's get out of here and go and rescue the girls."

We slowly walked down the back to the opposite end of the shipyard to where the 'Princess Sophie' was having her name changed, and then casually walked up between the last two boats, emerging just behind the guards. One of them spotted the movement behind him.

"Oi," he shouted at us. "Where the hell have you two just sprung from?"

"We were just looking at that lovely yacht at the end there, 'The Grey Gannet'," I answered, pointing at the yacht at the opposite end to the 'Princess Sophie'. "I don't suppose it's for sale, is it?" I asked him.

"No, it bloody isn't," he rudely replied. "Now sod off the pair of you, and you can take your bloody teasing wives with you."

We hastily collected the two girls, and instead of heading away from it, we headed straight back to our yacht, clambered aboard, started the engine and quickly left the yacht and boat yard of Nanaimo far behind us.

We headed due south on Captain Helena's instructions, and kept the throttle wide open, while at the same time keeping an eye on whether we were being followed. As far as we could tell, we weren't, and so we relaxed a bit when Richard suddenly exclaimed;

"Oh, the letter!"

We hadn't had time during our rapid departure to fill the girls in on what we'd discovered in the shipyard's office, or should I say what Richard discovered. We filled the girls in and then Richard handed the letter he'd photocopied to Helena.

"Well, I can tell you straightaway," she said. "This isn't Spanish. It looks like Portuguese to me, but I don't speak the language so I'm not sure."

"My Portuguese isn't too bad," said Sam. "Let's have a look."

Helena handed Sam the letter, and she read it through.

"It's just instructions to alter the 'Princess Sophie' by changing the name, adding dark blue coach lines to the hull, and replacing the existing sails with new ones showing a new set of letters and numbers. There's a totally unreadable scrawl of a signature at the bottom, but there's nothing here we didn't know already."

I'd been looking over Sam's shoulder and threw in my thoughts.

"Actually Sam, I think you're wrong."

She looked at me with a puzzled look on her face.

"There are two things here we didn't know before. One, this confirms without doubt that the instructions are coming from Portugal. We might have thought it, but we didn't know for sure until now."

"OK, I'll give you that one," said Sam. "What's the other thing?"

"Secondly," I said, "if my Portuguese is up to scratch, then that is a return address with a post office box number in the top left-hand corner, and if I'm right, that means we have an address for the forger, even if it is just a post office box."

"Hells teeth, you're right Michael," exclaimed Sam.

"It is a post office box and I completely missed it. It says '*Apartado cento e dezoito, Correio Al*'. That means post office box one hundred and eighteen at Albufeira post office."

"OK folks," said Helena. "Let's get this cruise ship back to its home port and return to Europe. I think a visit to Albufeira is definitely in order."

"What about me?" asked Richard. "Am I still needed?"

"Until death us do part, husband dearest," smiled Helena, and to prove her point, she gave Richard a short, but definite kiss on his lips, accompanied by her great smile.

Richard just said, "Ooh."

And then he smiled as well.

Chapter Eleven

Back in the Algarve we decided to use my villa as our base. Sam and I had shared the master bedroom for several months now, and that meant we still had two spare bedrooms left. Helena took one room and Richard the other. While they were both unpacking upstairs Sam told me that Helena had confided in her on the way home that she liked Richard a lot, but they weren't quite at that stage yet, if Sam could understand what she meant? Sam assured her that she did. Helena and Richard joined us, and the four of us sat in the garden by the pool with a pot of tea and a pile of bourbon biscuits and discussed what we were going to do next. The villa was thankfully very private, which was unusual for Quinta do Lago as most villas had quite small gardens for the size of the villas they encompassed. However, my villa had a considerable amount of lawn around it, which I have to say our Romanian gardeners kept beautifully mowed and watered, so our conversations were quite secure providing nobody was pointing a long-range microphone at us, and I doubted that at this stage in the investigation the opposition were even aware of our existence.

"OK boss," I asked Helena. "What's our next move, then?"

"Well I've already spoken to Kurt, who has now spoken to Paulo at the Portuguese GNR, and they have given me permission to put a discreet watch on the post office box in Albufeira. The box is unfortunately inside the post office which is quite small, so we've set up a long-range camera aimed at the box, from an upstairs window in one of the apartments opposite which is not let at the moment. We've also got two plain clothes four-man teams on the ground to form a box around whoever collects the post, and then hopefully follow them to their base."

"Can I make a suggestion based on what Richard said he'd do if he was running this scam?" I asked. "He said the Mediterranean would be the ideal base as we know they've been shifting counterfeit euros, but we know they've also been printing counterfeit sterling, so why don't we pay a visit to the boatyards of the UK first and see if we can get any leads that way. Searching the UK's boatyards for dodgy sterling transactions should be a lot easier than searching all over Europe's boatyards for dodgy euros."

"I agree," said Sam. "But surely we'd know about any big sales using counterfeit. If it was my boatyard and I'd just been done for a couple of million then I'd be straight on to the police, and surely, they'd tell Interpol, and that includes us now."

"You're forgetting one big thing Sam," said Helena. "Police forces the world over are sadly all the same! If a boatyard in say Kent gets turned over for your two million, then of course they'll report it firstly to the Kent police, who will tell the victims they're doing everything possible in their investigation, which of course they will be. Except for the one thing that will probably help them the most. What they won't do is ask for help. Like all police forces the world over, they'll try to solve it themselves rather than admit defeat and call in help from other UK forces or international forces such as Interpol. It's exactly the same in the States. The local sheriff will always try and solve every crime himself before sharing it with the local police. The local police are then just as bad and they will take forever trying to solve it before asking for nationwide help from the FBI. If the big organizations are called in straight away we can usually help because we will have seen or heard about something similar happening somewhere else and be able to link them together. But it can often take months before we get to hear about a crime, and by then, of course, it's frequently too late and the birds have flown."

"So, what do you think?" asked Sam. "Is it worth trying the UK?"

"Yes, I think it is," answered Helena.

"Can I run something by you all?" I asked. "My thinking is that the majority of people that enjoy boating in yachts, both sail power and engine power, prefer good weather. So, let's rule out Scotland which is beautiful, but sadly the weather is highly unpredictable, so let's concentrate on England. I think the place to start is one that has a hell of a lot of boat yards, and where better to hide a stolen boat than amongst lots of other boats?"

"So where are you thinking?" asked Richard.

"My favorite holiday resort when I was a kid. The Norfolk Broads. There must be at least a hundred boatyards on the broads, and hundreds, maybe even thousands of boats sailing around. It must be the easiest place in the world to steal a boat using counterfeit as the payment method, and then change a stolen boat's name and sell it."

"You mean you could steal a boat on one Broad, and then sell it on another one the other end of the Broads, having changed its name overnight," suggested Sam.

"Exactly," I replied.

"Surely, you'd need time to alter it and then sell it?" said Richard. "Wouldn't that be a bit risky, you know, keeping it in the same area while all the work was done?"

"Well if it needed a lot of work, perhaps yes," I answered. "And in that case you'd have to sail it quite a distance as soon as possible. But smaller boats can easily and quickly be changed. For example, spray the hull blue instead of its existing white, and then glue a pre-prepared new name board in smart polished wood over the old name on the back. Job done. Like changing cars, with the right people it can probably be done overnight."

"You're right," mused Richard. "Thinking about it, it is that easy."

"And don't forget," I said. "If they've got a top forger in the team, he can easily forge new ownership documents in advance, so that even if the police do come calling, they can prove the boat is legally theirs."

"Where exactly are the Norfolk Broads?" asked Helena. "And how do we get there?"

"The nearest airport is Norwich," said Richard. "But I don't know if you can fly there direct from the Algarve."

"I've just looked it up on the internet while we've been talking," said Sam. "It is possible. There's a small airline that has one direct flight to Norwich a day."

"Well in that case," said Helena, "can you please book four tickets for tomorrow?"

"Oh, bloody hell," said Richard. "I thought if I got to go out in the field with you guys, it would be somewhere a bit more exotic. I mean your last case took you to Venice, the Costa del Sol in Spain, the Algarve in sunny Portugal, South Africa and the amazing Bahamas. What do I get? Flaming Norwich and the bloody Norfolk Broads. Can't we go and look for stolen yachts in Bali or the Maldives instead?" We all laughed, and then the girls headed back to the bedrooms to pack clothes while Richard and I booked plane tickets for Norwich and a hired car from Norwich airport.

The next morning, we were all ready to leave for the airport when Helena's mobile phone rang. She answered it, listened for a couple of minutes, and then cursed in Dutch while switching off her phone.

"Listen to this," she said. "That was the team watching the post office box in Albufeira. A man with a moustache, probably false, wearing a hat and sun glasses and carrying a black brief case just came into the post office. He unlocked the post office box and then opened his brief case. He then took all the letters from the post office box, took a large pre-addressed and stamped padded envelope from his briefcase, slipped all the correspondence from the post office box inside it, sealed it and then reposted the package to God knows where. We can't check the post because we haven't got a warrant, and we'll never get one before the box is emptied because we have no proof of anything untoward against anyone. No, that avenue of enquiry has just closed."

"Surely your observer's team can follow him back to his base," I suggested.

"You'd think so, wouldn't you?' asked Helena in a sarcastic voice. "Our man in the hat disappeared into a busy shop in some big mall called Algarve Shopping, but they never saw him come out. We now assume he put his hat, sunglasses, moustache and jacket in the briefcase, put on a different jacket taken from the briefcase, then left the briefcase behind and wandered out looking completely different. Our men said they did see a young woman emerge from the same shop a few minutes later with a big shopping bag which could easily have had the briefcase in it, but they couldn't be sure, and again they had no right to stop her or question her."

"The good news is that we know we're on the right lines at least," said Sam. "We just have to keep going, not getting discouraged, and keep smiling."

"We also now know that this team is very professional," said Helena. "And they take a lot of precautions in everything they do as a matter of standard procedure. We must assume they don't know at this stage that they're being followed, and yet they still go through strict precautions against being tailed. I'm afraid this isn't going to be that easy."

"Well let's all look on the bright side," I said. "We're all off to sunny Norwich."

Everyone just groaned.

Chapter Twelve

We left our own cars at the villa and ordered a large taxi that was big enough to get the four of us and all our luggage to the airport. We boarded the plane in Faro and the two girls sat together so they could natter about girlie things, whatever 'girlie things' were. Richard had been whining all the way over on the flight, and only stopped when I suggested he and Sam changed seats so that he was sitting with Helena, and I had Sam to myself for a while. When we landed in Norwich it was raining, which set Richard off again about how we could have been searching marinas in the sunny Maldives. We picked up the hire car, a large 4 x 4 which had enough room for all Richard's silver-colored tech cases as well as our normal luggage, and headed for our hotel which overlooked the main marina on Wroxham Broad. By the time we arrived it had stopped raining, so we unpacked, had some lunch and then went for a wander round the marina.

We split up and went from boatyard to boatyard asking if anyone had sold any boats and received counterfeit cash in payment. After visiting sixteen boatyards of varying sizes, I was starting to think this was a really silly idea. Then I came across William Chatsworth's boatyard. I would say Chatsworth was in his mid-sixties, still fairly trim in a smart open necked blue and white striped shirt and fawn colored trousers, and he had the usual weather-beaten face of most Norfolk folk. He was standing chatting with one of his older employees who was busy scraping down the bottom of the hull. Apparently, you have to do that fairly regularly as most boats on the broads, or anywhere else for that matter, pick up a fair amount of river scum, oxidation, barnacles etc. Anyway, I introduced myself to Mr. Chatsworth as a police consultant, and waved my Interpol ID briefly under his nose.

A Typical Norfolk Broads Marina

Pleasure Boats on the Norfolk Broads

"Good morning Mr. Chatsworth," I said. "We're investigating a number of boat thefts both here and abroad where the thieves have paid for their purchases with large amounts of counterfeit cash, and I wondered if you'd been affected in this way with any dodgy cash."

"No, sorry son, I haven't seen any counterfeit cash, at least not as far as I know."

"Well thank you for your time anyway Mr. Chatsworth," I said and turned to leave.

"I got done with a dodgy bank draft though. Does that count?" he asked.

"You bet it does," I replied. "If you don't mind can you give me some details?"

"Yeah. Sure. Well there was two of them, a married couple in their mid-forties I'd guess, both Welsh I'd say judging by their accents, and, well, they said they'd taken a liking to a second-hand yacht I'd just finished doing up. It wasn't massive, just a seventy-footer, a beautiful Fairline Squadron 78 it was, built in 2009 and customized for its previous owner. I'd picked it up in the south of France, and to be frank, I got it for a song, only 600,000 euros, but I could see it had an enormous amount of potential. Anyway, the lads gave it some tender loving care, and when it was finished, I advertised it for sale at £1.6 million. To cut a long story short, this couple said their names were Clive and Cynthia Martin by the way…where was I, Oh yes…as I was saying, they offered me £1.3 million, and said they'd pay the following day with a certified bankers draft."

"What day of the week was that Mr. Chatsworth, can you remember?"

"Oh, I remember all right. It was a Thursday, and I said to them, they'd need to be back with the bank draft by midday because the bank closes at lunchtime on Fridays."

"And they were back on Friday?" I asked.

"Yes, they were back, but not till nearly three o'clock, by which time the bank had closed and the staff had all gone home. They were full of apologies, and they then said Mr. Fitzgerald, the bank manager, had been tied up with another customer, and they'd only just got out of the bank as the staff locked the front door. But to be honest, I wasn't concerned because Mr. Martin had a certified bank draft for one and point three million pounds with him, issued and signed by my own bank manager, Mr. Fitzgerald, at my own bank."

"And I suppose you accepted the draft in payment, and then they happily sailed away with your yacht into the unknown?"

"Too bloody right they did. It wasn't until Monday morning when I took the bank draft round to my local branch to pay it in, that the cashier called the Manager over. He always has to authorize bank drafts, and we've gone through this procedure several times over the years. Anyway, he took one look at the draft and asked me to go into his office where he told me he hadn't issued any bank drafts that week, and as he was the only person in the bank that had access to that facility, he'd know. Unfortunately, I had in his opinion been well and truly done by the bastards, and he said that the bank draft was a truly excellent fake, or a counterfeit if you prefer, and if he didn't know better because he signed them, he would have happily accepted it as being genuine."

"No chance of getting your money back, or even the yacht?"

"You tell me. The money's gone, but I guess I may be lucky and you'll find the yacht for me, but it's been over two weeks now and the local police, who've incidentally got the counterfeit draft, say they've got no leads. I suppose it was them that called you guys in?"

"Sadly, no Mr. Chatsworth. We knew nothing about this until you just told me."

I spent the next hour with William Chatsworth in his office, where he gave me details of the yacht and everything he could remember about Clive and Cynthia Martin, although we both thought that was certainly not their real names. I rang Helena on her mobile, and then Sam and finally Richard, and we all agreed to meet back at the hotel.

I'd been covering the Wroxham area, Sam had been to Potter Heigham & Hickling, Helena had been to Great Yarmouth & Oulton Broad and Richard had been asking questions around the Reedham & Brundall area. I filled the other three in on what happened with Mr. Chatsworth, and Richard said he'd had a case with a small boat being sold for ten thousand in forged fifty-pound notes. Sam had two cases, one in Hickling with counterfeit cash, and the other like mine, a bigger transaction using a counterfeit bank draft. This one for seven hundred and fifty thousand pounds. Helena said she was extremely worried by this new development.

"What this means is the counterfeiters have now upped their game considerably in that instead of trying to convince people to accept great piles of cash, which always looks a bit suspicious, they are now offering counterfeit certified bank drafts for the bigger deals. So good in fact, the men authorized to issue them at the banks couldn't tell the difference."

"How difficult is it to forge a bank draft, and then spot it?" asked Sam.

"Well," began Helena, "in an ideal world, if someone wants to pay you by bank draft, you should ideally go to the bank with them, and insist on watching the bank manager or teller issue the draft and sign it in front of you. Never wait outside the bank or the Manager's office. Always insist on going in. We had a case of some very good forged bank drafts circulating in Rotterdam, Delft and Den Haag or The Hague as you English call it, where the scammers set up various meetings with numerous different bank managers for fake reasons, and all just in case the sellers, it was cars in this case, wanted to come to the bank with them. The scammer took the seller into the bank with him, he was all smiles and niceness, but unbeknown to the seller he always had the fake draft on him right from the start. He then simply took it out of his pocket to give to the seller just before leaving the bank, claiming that he'd just been given it by the manager. How were you supposed to know the draft had been in his pocket all the time, and that he and the manager had actually been talking about him and his wife taking out the bank's private health insurance."

"God, it seems impossible to protect yourself against these people," said Sam.

"What concerns me the most," said Helena, "is that if our forger is now producing bank drafts good enough to fool bank managers, who all have training in spotting forgeries, then they must be really good. If they're really good then they'll use them for even higher value scams such as property, land, private jets. You name it."

"Can we get our hands on the bank draft dumped on Chatsworth, or Sam's one?" I asked. "You never know, they might give us some leads."

"I'll go and see the Norfolk Police and see if they'll cooperate with me," said Helena. "They don't usually say no when they come face to face with a high-ranking Interpol officer, and I imagine that will particularly be the case when faced with the Head of European Operations. Come with me by all means, but can I ask you all to wait outside in the car. I don't want to intimidate them with numbers. My rank should hopefully be enough."

Helena disappeared inside the Headquarters of the Norfolk Constabulary as the police of Norfolk are called, and she emerged about fifteen minutes later with both bank drafts in her hand. She handed one to me to have a look at and I have to say, it was a beautiful piece of work. Top quality cream-colored linen paper with a silver band through the center. A clear and crisp watermark, the banks logo beautifully embossed and even the branches own rubber stamp on top of the Manager's signature. It was good enough to fool anyone who didn't know better. The other draft was just as good, but raised against a different bank.

"So, what do we do now?' I asked.

"Can I make a suggestion?" asked Richard. "I think we should pack up shop here and drive down to Greenwich. I've got the facilities there to check the paper, the inks used, the embossing implements used etc. Hopefully that may provide some new leads."

"Of course, husband dearest," said Helena. "Your wish is our command."

"You know once we really are married," announced Richard, "You really must stop calling me husband dearest, and start referring to me as O Lord and Master."

"Of course, dear," replied Helena. "But only once we're married."

Having checked out of our hotel, we set off for Greenwich, and once we'd arrived it was late evening and Helena, Sam and myself booked into our usual hotel whenever we were staying in south London. Richard bade us farewell for the time being, got a quick peck on the cheek from Sam, a slightly longer one from Helena, and headed home as he only lived in Blackheath, just three miles away. We all met up again at 10:30 a.m. the following morning in Stephen's office, with Paul joining us in person and Kurt joining us on a secure video link from Interpol's office in Geneva, where he was involved on a different case involving something he called interbank fraud, whatever the hell that was. Apparently, Richard had been in his department since 8.00 am and had called in two of his assistants to help him. They had some news for us.

"Firstly, I traced the papers being used for the bank drafts. The cream colored linen paper is German, produced in A1 sized sheets by a government-licensed paper mill in Frankfurt, and seventy reams of it were stolen about four months ago, and never found.

"It's a similar story with the white paper, although that is French and again comes from a government-licensed paper mill just outside Nantes. Again, it is produced in A1 sized sheets, and this time over two hundred and fifty reams of it were stolen, also about four months ago. As with the German theft, the paper was never recovered. Working out the total amount of paper stolen, and the approximate size of the average bank draft, then allowing for wastage, I estimate our forgers can produce approximately one and a quarter million bank drafts using the paper they already have."

"Nice work Richard," said Stephen. "Any idea where it's gone, or is that asking too much at this early stage?"

"Yes, it is a bit early sir, but I do have one or two clues, and there is quite a lot of information on the various inks used."

"Sorry to have interrupted your flow Richard," said Stephen. "Please, carry on."

At that moment there was a knock on the door, and Carol from the canteen brought in a tray with tea and biscuits on, which she put on the table in front of Paul, and then left.

"Oh, I see," he said. "Am I mother again?"

"I'm saying nothing," said Sam, and everyone giggled as Paul began pouring.

"Please carry on Richard," requested Helena. "I'm all ears."

Richard just smiled at the woman he was so obviously smitten with, coughed briefly, and then carried on speaking.

"I got in touch with the company in Frankfurt that makes the cream paper, and they have very few customers for this particular paper. As it's used for bank drafts its distribution is highly regulated and controlled, although they will always sell it to a new customer providing they check out. I asked them if they'd had anyone asking especially for that paper and they said they did have an enquiry about a year ago from a company in Spain, but as they didn't have the necessary licenses they couldn't supply them as it was a paper made especially for banks."

"Very interesting," mused Paul.

"I did the same with the French company, and they said much the same as the Frankfurt mill. They'd had a telephone enquiry from a Spanish company, but as they don't sell to non-banking organizations, they said a very definite no. They thought that was about a year ago as well, and before you ask, neither company had a return phone number or company name. Just a Spanish company, although the German manager I spoke to said he thought the contact said he was calling from Seville, but that could of course be untrue."

"You said you might have some news on the inks?" said Kurt listening in over the video link. "I don't suppose there is a Spanish link there by any chance?"

"Funny you should say that Kurt," said Richard. "There is."

"Tell us more," I urged.

"What we're talking about here is printer's ink, and that is very different to the ink you put in fountain pens or biros. Printer's ink is more like a thick ointment in consistency, or like artist's oil paint, you know the stuff I mean, you buy it in tubes. Anyway, the red printer's ink used on the cream bank drafts is a custom color especially made by a company in Worcester, here in the UK especially for the bank, which is also based here in the UK. Now I remember this next bit from my college days."

"Oh, do get on with it Richard," said a very impatient Stephen.

"You carry on at your own pace, Richard," said Helena. "I think it's very interesting, and you shouldn't let the nasty man bully you."

"Don't say anything Stephen," I whispered quietly. "They're in love."

"Oh, heaven help us," he replied,

"I knew I shouldn't have let him go with you."

"As I was saying," said Richard, "colors all have something called a pantone number, and that determines the precise shade and depth of the ink's color, in this case PMS 1795. This stands for Pantone Matching System, by the way. The bank is the only company they make that specific shade for, and nobody else in seven years has ever ordered that color although they do make it available should anyone ever ask. After all, it's basically just red printer's ink."

"I sense a 'but' coming," said Paul.

"Correct," said Richard. "About three months ago, they received a telephone order for thirty liters of red printer's ink, and the guy ordering it on the phone specified the exact self-same pantone number – PMS 1795."

"Did they get a delivery address from him?" asked Paul.

"No, they asked for one, but the man said he'd collect it when it was ready. He did, however, leave a mobile phone number they could ring him back on and let him know when it was ready to collect. It was a Spanish mobile and I got the number from their records, but I'm afraid it is no longer connected."

"Did the man sign for anything when he collected the ink?" asked Sam.

"Yes," replied Richard. "He signed for it and it's more or less a scribble, but having put it through the computers, the best I can come up with is Anibal Henriques."

"The phone number well may have been Spanish," said Sam. "But that is very definitely a Portuguese name, not Spanish at all. What's the chances that we've got another one of these international crime thingies on our hands?"

"You mean, perhaps," I said, "it's the proverbial 'Don't shit on your own doorstep' brigade. It maybe they do everything through Spain, although they're actually based in Portugal, probably Faro according to Stephen's original brief. I would think they more than likely sent an underling to collect the printer's ink, and when he was asked to sign for it, he didn't think and automatically signed his own name."

"I think you're probably right Michael," said Kurt. "The more I hear about this, the more I am convinced this is an operation running out of Portugal using front men, and grunts as Michael calls them from Portugal and in numerous different countries."

"But why based in Portugal?" asked Sam. "You never did tell us."

"For the reason Kurt has just said," replied Stephen. "As Michael so poetically phrased it. "You never shit on your own doorstep."

"Interpol have had numerous reports of high end car and yacht thefts using counterfeit currency here in the UK, France, Belgium Holland, Spain, Greece, Italy, Canada and the USA, but nothing in Portugal, which should be high on the list as it has one of the best and richest marinas in Europe at Vilamoura."

"OK," Sam responded. "I can see that, and what you say makes really good sense, but why did you nickname him the Faro Forger even before you knew all this?"

"Oh that," said Stephen. "Well, it wasn't me that gave him the nickname actually, that was good old Bert. In fact, it all goes back about three years, when Bert Connick, an old lag, sorry Helena, that's a term we use for people who've done time in prison. Anyway, this old lag Bert, had been a part time informer for us when he was in between jobs so to speak, and at the time he'd just completed a five year stretch for passing counterfeit. As he was leaving the prison after his latest stretch, Bert said to one of the guards, just in a simple throwaway passing comment, that he wished he'd had counterfeit produced by the Faro Forger, then he'd never have been caught, as his product was just as good as the real thing. Anyway, the prison guard just told Bert to sling his hook, and never to darken their doorstep again. The guard never thought about Bert's comment and never mentioned it to anyone. Bert settled back into normal life and he was even a regular attendee at the Salvation Army. He was doing fine. Then about a year ago the prison guard got nattering in a pub after his shift one night, and the subject of top quality counterfeit came up. He straightaway remembered what Bert had said and the following morning he mentioned it to the DCI who was visiting the prison, who said he'd make a few enquiries. Two days later poor Bert was found dead in an alley with his throat cut and a large cork stuffed in his mouth. The underworld's way of saying keep your mouth shut. That action alone told us that there had to be some truth in the matter, and that in all probability there really was a Faro Forger, who, to use Bert's words, 'made product just as good as the real thing'."

"And if there wasn't a Faro Forger, why kill Bert?" I mused.

"Exactly," said Stephen.

Chapter Thirteen

We'd decided the next step was to do a bit more work on the paper and ink enquiries. Sam and I made appointments with the papermakers in Frankfurt and Nantes, as well as the ink manufacturers in Worcester. As we were in the UK already, Sam and I drove to Worcester early the following morning. We had an early afternoon meeting with Mr. Hugh Duffy, the company's Managing Director and CEO. We showed him both our police and Interpol IDs and he agreed to help us in any way he could.

We were with him for nearly two hours as Mr. Duffy talked us through his specialist subject, security printing. As well as manufacturing their own range of inks, his company were specialists in the field of security printing, and he explained that they dealt with many areas of security printing including banknotes, cheques , passports, tamper evident labels, product authentication, stock certificates, postage stamps and identity cards. Sam and I both asked what must have seemed like pretty basic questions, but Hugh Duffy loved talking about his subject and happily explained to us the wonders of his trade. He said the main goal of security printing is fairly obvious I guess and that is to prevent forgery, tampering, or counterfeiting. Mr. Duffy explained that security printers now have many weapons in their arsenal including special papers, watermarks, intaglio printing, geometric lathe work, micro printing, optically variable color-changing inks, holograms, security threads, magnetic ink, serial numbers, anti-copying marks, prismatic coloration, false-positive testing, fluorescent dyes, registration of features on both sides, various electronic devices, thermo-chromatic ink and latent images. Sam and I listened intently as Hugh Duffy got more and more excited about all these various techniques, and when we eventually left him we felt we were incredibly well versed in the world of security printing.

The first thing Hugh Duffy mentioned in his list was the use of special papers, and during the next forty-eight hours at our meetings in Frankfurt and Nantes, Sam and I learnt about the myriad of different papers used to produce currency and cheques the world over. It turned out that most banknotes are made of heavy paper, almost always from cotton fibers for strength and durability, and in some cases linen or specialty colored or forensic fibers are added to give the paper added individuality and protect against counterfeiting. Some countries, including Canada, Nigeria, Romania, Mexico, Canada, New Zealand, Israel, Singapore, Malaysia, the UK and Australia now produce plastic banknotes, which helps to improve longevity and it also allows the inclusion of a small transparent window, which is just a few millimeters in size, as an added security feature that is really difficult to reproduce using common counterfeiting techniques. We returned to the UK feeling we now knew the subject matter very well, but we weren't sure if our new knowledge was going to help in our search for the Faro Forger.

After breakfast Sam and I joined Stephen, Paul, Richard and Helena in Stephen's office, with Kurt again joining us via video link.

"So where do we go from here?" I asked. "My little brain has run out of ideas."

"Likewise," said Sam. "Is there any new information we can follow up on?"

"As it happens," interjected Kurt's voice. "There is. A report came in overnight of another yacht theft, a big one this time, but fortunately for us, the owner had accidentally left his iPhone on-board, and he has given us permission to track the phone, and therefore track the yacht."

"Great," said Helena. "Where, what, when, how etc.?" she then queried.

"The yacht was stolen from Puerto Banus, the marina just outside Marbella on the Costa del Sol in southern Spain," said Kurt.

"We have been tracking it for over fourteen hours now and as far as we can tell at this stage, it looks like they're heading for the southern coast of Italy, but they could go further and head for

Malta, Sicily or even on into Greece or Turkey. Obviously, we don't know where their final destination is at this stage. I am assuming Stephen, that you will be happy to let Interpol continue to use Richard's technical skills for the duration of the operation as well. I will pick up Richard's salary and expenses while he is with us."

Richard beamed across the table at Sam, Helena and myself:

"Do I have a choice Kurt?" asked Stephen grumpily. Then smiling, he said, "Yes, of course Kurt, that will be fine. Can I just ensure Richard's team get a thorough briefing before he heads off again?"

"Of course, and thank you. OK, well in that case," continued Kurt. "I suggest the Fantastic Four head out to Italy straight away, and aim to be there to meet the yacht. I am putting Interpol's new Gulf Stream and its crew at your disposal Helena, for the duration of this operation, and I suggest you make sure you get to wherever the yacht is heading before it does."

"I am assuming Kurt," I began. "That you want us to track the people meeting the yacht and see where they lead us, rather than repossess the yacht?"

"Yes, I do, and I have to say, it took a lot of persuasion to get the yacht's owner to agree to let us see this thing through, but I think he liked the idea of having Interpol owe him one as he called it. Pieter Van Riesbrink is a Dutch billionaire financier, and his yacht is called the 'Nefertiti', after the ancient Egyptian queen, and I have to say it is a rather special boat. Over sixty meters in length, it was built to his own design in the early nineties and it has absolutely everything you could possibly want on board. There is even a shiny ebony black six-foot-long concert grand piano sitting in the main lounge."

"Don't these large yachts have a crew on board at all times?" asked Sam.

"Oh yes, and the 'Nefertiti' has such a crew. A permanent crew of ten people to be precise. The boat was silently boarded around three am, and the crew were all encouraged to stay asleep with some form of gas or chloroform. The thieves then took the yacht out of Puerto Banus under the cover of darkness, and the crew were later dumped out at sea in a life raft, all still unconscious. They were all safely picked up by the Spanish coastguard around 8.00 am, but they'd seen or heard nothing and were no help at all. Of course, by the time they were picked up the yacht had long disappeared who knows where. Nobody was hurt, so as far as the Spanish are concerned this is now just property theft. They know nothing about the bigger picture, and I have no intention of confiding in them."

"Any idea how much the yacht is worth?" I asked.

"Well according to its owner, he was aiming to sell it later this year for around eighteen million euros, but he also said it is insured for over twenty-five million."

"I guess he's in no hurry to get it back then?" Sam laughed with a slightly cynical tone in her voice.

"You said just now that they were heading for southern Italy, but wherever they're going, wouldn't a yacht like this stick out like a sore thumb. There can't be that many yachts like the 'Nefertiti' out there bobbing about on the waves."

"You'd be surprised at just how many of these incredible yachts there are sailing round the Med. As for your question Sam, well it's all a question of disguise. I'm pretty sure, they must have a dry dock or a boatyard somewhere that they can take the yacht and stick it under cover for a few weeks while they set about changing its appearance. Paint the hull and the funnel a different color, obviously change the name, add some extra deck work to change its outline, so on and so forth. I spoke to Fairline, one of your UK yacht building companies, and they said there are hundreds of boatyards round the Med that could do the work. Changing the color is an obvious thing to do, but they suggested putting a different funnel shape on to change the outline, plus some extra deck work and railings, and when it set sail again, nobody would know that it used to be the 'Nefertiti'."

"Did your contact offer any thoughts on where the necessary work was most likely to be undertaken?" I asked.

"Yes, he said if it was him, he'd head for Tunisia, Greece or Turkey," replied Kurt. "And at this stage they could be heading for any of those three. On the other hand, it could be Malta, Libya or Cyprus. We've absolutely no way of knowing until they get to wherever the hell it is they're going."

"The iPhone you mentioned," said Helena. "Is it liable to run out of power?"

"No. Fortunately for us, the phone is on charge in the owner's bedroom drawer. Apparently, all the bedroom drawers in the various staterooms have phone chargers built into them would you believe, so that any light emitted from the phone while on charge doesn't keep them awake at night."

"Good grief," said Stephen. "How the other half lives!"

"I take your point Stephen," said Kurt, "but what it does mean is that the phone's battery won't go flat, and because it's tucked away in a drawer, the phone is also unlikely to be found. Look, I've sent Interpol's Gulfstream and its crew to Biggin Hill aerodrome in Kent. Helena knows the crew quite well, and I've also had all sorts of technical goodies put on board for Richard to play with, along with the relevant operating manuals. Please use the three-man crew, although one of them is in fact a woman, in any way you think that they might be helpful. As well as being very experienced pilots, they're also highly trained Interpol operatives with all manner of skills and techniques at their disposal. They're brilliant and I promise you, you'll find them extremely helpful. Can I suggest you all get down to Biggin Hill and board the plane as soon as possible? Just make sure you get to wherever the yacht is going before they do, see who meets it and track them. I'm sorry, but I've got to go as I've got another meeting in Geneva, but call me anytime if you need me."

We chatted over one or two details for another thirty minutes or so while Richard went down to his department and the men he was leaving in charge until this particular investigation was over. We then drove to Biggin Hill aerodrome in Kent where we found the Gulfstream and its crew waiting for us. It was a G650ER, the latest in the range, and more than adequate for Interpol's needs. The jet had no external markings to identify it as anything other than a rich businessman's plaything, and Helena had decided that that was going to be my role if and when anybody asked whose plane it was? We got airborne with our three-man crew – the pilot, a second officer, and a stewardess. As Kurt had said, they were all Interpol officers and would be available to us should their help be needed. George Copeland, our pilot, was also an Interpol officer with the rank of Senior Inspector, and he informed us that the 'Nefertiti' had just passed Tunisia and Malta, and looked to be heading towards the Greek Island of Crete. Helena asked George to head for Crete and radio ahead with a flight plan. We could always change it if necessary. Although Heraklion was the main airport on Crete, George radioed ahead and obtained permission for us to land at Chania, the nearer and smaller airport in the west of the island. George was fairly certain Crete was the destination, and he'd assured us that if the 'Nefertiti' was heading somewhere beyond Crete, then they wouldn't be taking the course and heading they'd taken.

Interpol's G650 Gulfstream

The Gulfstream's Interior

As soon as we'd landed at Chania airport, we picked up a couple of hire cars – a silver Ford Mondeo and a white Ford Focus, and we had just finished putting all Richard's gear in the boot of the Mondeo when Colin O'Donnell, the Gulfstream's co-pilot, second officer and also an Inspector, shouted down to me from the top steps of the plane.

"Slight problem Michael. The 'Nefertiti' has turned due South and looks to be heading for a small island, but according to my maps and charts, it's uninhabited."

"How far away is it?" I shouted back.

"I guess if you put your foot down, about a ten-minute drive."

The four of us sped up what we were doing, jumped into the Mondeo with myself at the wheel, and George and Colin jumped in the Focus, George driving and Colin navigating. They took the lead and I followed. We had decided that Jo Sylvester, our very delectable stewardess, a sergeant with Interpol and also a highly trained operative should stay with the aircraft in case anyone got a bit nosey.

The island in question was in fact called Agioi Theodoroi, fortunately for us located north west of Chania. It was very small, had just one building on it, a small white concrete church reached by a solitary track leading up from the southern beach and as far as we could tell, the island was totally uninhabited. We were all lying on our stomachs on the flat roof of the Hotel Minerva peering across the bay at Agioi Theodoroi island through binoculars. The Gulfsteam was incredibly well equipped with all manner of equipment and George had mentioned that it included in its inventory four pairs of Canon 18 x 50 IS all-weather binoculars. These, he told us, were ideal for surveillance work, and we brought a couple of pairs with us. They had eighteen times magnification, apparently the first number stands for the amount of magnification Colin said, and the IS in the title stands for image stabilization, which is really important. The stabilization electronics tend to make them a bit heavier than standard binoculars, but that is irrelevant if you're using them on the top of a tripod, which we were. Colin never did tell me what the second number meant!

The 'Nefertiti' had now turned off all its lights, both external and internal, plunging the yacht into total darkness. I could just about make out the yacht's outline by the minimal light of the half-moon that night, and from what little I could see it was about half a mile to a mile out to sea, and appeared to have come to a complete halt and dropped anchor. I had the distinct feeling we were probably in for a very long night. It was now late evening, and the light was fading fast.

"I don't suppose you've got a boat of some sort tucked away in your flying Noah's Ark?" I asked George. "I would love to get out to the island and have a closer look at what they're up to, but I really don't fancy swimming."

"As it happens Michael, we do have a small Rib in the Gulfstream's hold. It's not massive, but it should take four of us with no problem. Why don't Colin and I take the two girls back to the plane, so that Helena can then liaise with Kurt and let him know what's happening, we can then hook the Rib onto the tow bar of the Mondeo and bring it back."

"Ribs arc thosc small inflatable boats, aren't they?" asked Sam. "If I remember rightly their engines are really noisy. Especially at night, which it will be by the time you get back."

"Interpol only buys and uses the best," George reassured Sam. "The engines are well-padded and have great silencers attached. They're not silent, but they are incredibly quiet."

"Well I need to talk to Kurt anyway," said Helena, "So that makes a lot of sense. Come on then Sam, let's get back to the plane and leave the men to their night maneuvers."

The aircraft was only a ten-minute car ride away, and George and Colin were back about half an hour later towing a matt black Rib on a matt black trailer behind them. The Rib, which stands for Rigid Inflatable Boat, was 5 meters in length, and everything about it was matt black, including the engine casing. The engine also had an additional large padded fiber glass box over it which Colin said kept the sound level to an absolute minimum, and both George and Colin had apparently been trained in the use of Ribs as well as piloting aircraft. George threw black roll neck jumpers and black balaclava style hats to Richard and myself saying,

"Stick these on guys, if you don't want to be seen."

"How the hell did you two get into doing this for a living?" I asked getting dressed.

Chania, Crete

The Small Island of Agioi Theodoroi

"Oh, well I'd been working as a mail pilot in Australia for several years," said George, "And Colin joined the same company a year later, and we hit it off straight away. It was good money for very basic flying work and as both of us were single we had no ties to prevent us doing whatever we wanted. As you may have gathered by the way, I'm a Brit, born and bred in Bristol, but our Colin here is from Dublin in the Emerald Isle, and he's very proud of his Irish heritage."

"Oh, that I am, begorrah, begosh," laughed Colin, who had no Irish accent at all.

"Colin and I then went to South Africa after our Australian contracts finished and we were working the mail planes there two years later when we ran into Kurt," continued George.

"He was still a Captain then and involved on some long- term Interpol job based in Durban, and he needed to fly all over the place intercepting mail for some reason or other. Anyway, when our contract with the mail company was finished, we'd worked with Kurt on and off for nearly two years, and he'd got to know us both pretty well. To cut a long story short, he approached us both and asked if we'd be interested in working for Interpol in South Africa. Our main job would still be flying, but we'd also need to train for over a year in several other areas including driving boats, high speed car handling, unarmed combat, various covert activities we can't mention and handling firearms. It all sounded much more exciting than delivering mail, so we both said yes. We've been with Interpol nearly five years now, and when Kurt was recently promoted to his current job and needed a full time crew for the Gulfstream he offered the job to us. We jumped at the chance, and he has kept the two of us and Jo together as a permanent team ever since. We love it."

"So, Michael," asked Colin. "What's the plan?"

"Well at the moment we can't see a damn thing," I replied. "So I suggest we head out to the island as quietly as possible, hide the Rib as best we can off the beach, and then head up to the north side so we can watch what's happening with the 'Nefertiti', if anything."

"Whatever you say boss," said Colin.

"Just so there's no doubt by the way," said George. "Kurt has made it very clear to us that although we may have Interpol rank, we're all very much a team and that we should listen to you as you seem to have a knack for this sort of work, and that's fine by us."

"Let's go then," said Colin.

We loaded our equipment into a couple of black rucksacks Colin had brought back with him – the binoculars and their two tripods, several small electronic tracking devices of Richard's and a powerful two-way radio headset linking us to Helena back on the Gulfstream. George started the engine, and we set off. He was right, it wasn't totally silent, but it was damn close. The journey only took about five or six minutes, and having landed on the sandy beach, we pulled the boat up and hid it as best we could among the rocks, piling a few carefully on top to help with camouflaging it. We then loaded ourselves up with all the equipment and slowly headed up the track towards the small church. It was now pitch black and incredibly quiet. As we reached the church at the brow of the small hill in the center of the island, we could hear people talking, which we assumed was sound drifting ashore from conversations on board the 'Nefertiti'. George indicated for us all to crouch down low, and we then slowly crept forward for about ten or eleven agonizingly long minutes until we suddenly found ourselves on the top of a fifty-foot-high cliff. We stopped perfectly still and just listened for a moment or two. We then realized that the sound of talking wasn't drifting ashore from the 'Nefertiti', but was coming directly from the foot of the cliff below us. I indicated that I wanted to creep sideways a bit and see if we could spot anything. Colin slowly and quietly led the way, with me following behind him, while George and Richard stayed where they were on the top of the cliff.

There wasn't much in the way of rocks or bushes to hide behind, so we crept backwards away from the cliff edge first of all, then moved very slowly and very quietly about thirty or forty feet to our right, and then crept forward where the cliff stuck out slightly, and then we crawled to the cliff edge again and looked back and down to our left. What we saw caused us both to draw a deep breath. There was a gigantic hole about forty-foot-wide and forty-foot-high in the side of the cliff creating a vast cave, and the 'Nefertiti' was no longer out at sea, but had silently cruised to the mouth of the entrance and was now immediately below us, slowly and gently sliding stern first into the cave. From the little we could see, it was definitely not a natural cave, but had obviously been hewn or blasted out of the rock, and we could just about make out a concrete harbor style wall running along the inside of the cave. The 'Nefertiti' was very slowly disappearing inside, no lights showing, either on the yacht or inside the cave, and no engine noise whatsoever, just some very calm and very gentle talking. There were about ten men milling about down below, all gently pulling the yacht into the cave with ropes. One of the men was directing everybody with lots of arm waving and quiet instructions, and we assumed he was the boss.

Colin tapped me on the shoulder and pointed down to our right. He'd just spotted a fairly large and expensive looking smart black speed boat tied up, which I hadn't noticed at all, and we both assumed that was how the men who were not part of the 'Nefertiti's' pirate crew had reached the cave. I gently gestured to Colin that we should go back up and we very quietly edged backwards. Once we were out of sight and hopefully out of hearing range I shared my thoughts.

"We need Richard to get at least one of his trackers on that speedboat," I whispered. "We can't put a tracker on a car at this stage as there's no car here, but if we can track the speedboat, we may find a car at the end of it."

"Agreed," said Colin. "Let's get back."

We crawled back to Richard and filled both him and George in on what we'd found.

"If you don't mind Michael," said George, "Colin and I should handle placing the tracker. We've been highly trained in this covert stuff by Kurt and his team, and no insult intended, but I know you two haven't. Besides, we need Richard safely back here to operate the bugs, and we need you to stay alive and coordinate everything. If you don't mind, leave it to us. Richard can show us which buttons to press etc., and you can bring Helena and Sam up to date via the radio."

I agreed straight away, delighted at not having to return to the cave. Richard showed George and Colin how to activate his bugs, and how to attach them to the underside of the speedboat. It meant one of them was going to have to get wet, and Colin demanded that it should be his job as he said it was only fair on poor old George as Colin was the youngest. By all of six weeks apparently! They set off, disappeared into the darkness and didn't return for what seemed like hours. I kept checking my watch, but every time I looked only a few minutes had passed. About twenty minutes later the pair of them quietly returned, both drenched through.

"How did it go?" I whispered.

"Let's get out of here first," said George, and we all quickly made our way back down to the beach and our waiting Rib. We pulled the rocks off of it, and quickly and quietly carried it into the water. We pushed off and as we quietly drove back towards the beach Colin filled us in on what had happened.

"We slowly climbed down the cliff, roughly where you and I were earlier, about fifty feet to the right of the cave entrance, and then George noticed one of the men still on the 'Nefertiti' was holding a handgun. Having seen that we decided we simply couldn't risk being caught, and it was going to be safest for both of us, and for you guys as well, if we remained unseen, and so we approached their speedboat underwater the whole way. When we got there, George handed me both bugs, and I attached and activated them exactly as Richard had showed me. We went back to where we'd originally entered the water, and we then decided to hang around listening for a few minutes to see if we could pick up on any conversation or recognize anything being said."

"They were all speaking in a foreign language," said George. "And I assumed at first that being in Crete they'd all be speaking Greek. But it didn't sound at all like Greek, and I know it wasn't French, Spanish or Italian as I speak a bit of each. I also don't think it was German, that's far too aggressive a language and I'm sure I'd recognize it if I heard it."

"I think it was Portuguese," said Colin. "I heard one of them say '*Segunda-feira*' and that's Monday in Portuguese. The boss man, or at least the guy we assume was the boss then said something, and another one replied, "'*Terça-feira*', and I know that's Tuesday in Portuguese. I don't know a lot of Portuguese, but I do know the really important stuff like how to order a beer obviously, but I also know my numbers and my days of the week."

"That all ties in very nicely," I mused aloud. "Great stuff guys."

We arrived back at the beach, loaded the Rib onto its trailer and then drove back to the Gulfstream where we put the Rib and its trailer back in the hold. We gave the girls a briefing, and then ate the meal Jo had made for us all, as Richard watched his iPad and waited for his tracking bugs on the speedboat to kick in and start moving.

Chapter Fourteen

We didn't have long to wait.

"The speedboat's just started moving," said Richard suddenly.

"Which way is it headed?" I asked.

"Back towards Chania and us," answered Richard.

"If we jump in one of the cars," said Sam, "couldn't we race to meet them, then turn and follow them along the coast, and as they come ashore we can see if they have a car?"

"Great idea. Let's take both cars and all go," I suggested.

"You too, Jo."

We quickly locked up the plane, jumped into the two cars following Sam's suggestion. We raced west as fast as possible to try and get alongside the speedboat, and once we were in position we turned through 180 degrees and headed back in the direction we'd just come from. We were all doing this on Richard's instructions as none of us, including Richard could actually see the boat. All we had to go on was the little flashing red blob on Richard's iPad screen. I was driving the Mondeo with Richard in the front alongside me giving me directions; Sam and Helena sat in the back. George, Colin and Jo were all in the Focus following us. Richard said that the speedboat was about three hundred yards out to sea and was following the coastline. We expected it to turn inland when it reached Chania, but instead it just kept going. We were now heading northwards towards the top of the spit of land on which Chania airport was located on the east side. Richard suddenly gave a little "Whoop".

"It's slowing right down and turning inland. According to my map, it appears to be heading for Stavros Beach."

It was now well after midnight as we raced ahead and arrived just in time to see the speedboat stop and tie up on the harbor arm. About six men got out of the speedboat which I assumed meant the other four of the ten we had counted earlier had stayed with the ‘Nefertiti’. There were just two cars parked on the sandy beach, an old maroon colored BMW 5 Series and a much newer silver Toyota Land Cruiser 4 x 4. Five of the men walked passed the cars and headed towards a local bar which was firmly closed. However, one of the five had door keys. He unlocked the bar, turned on some lights and they all went inside. The remaining man opened the driver’s door of the BMW, threw something onto the front seat, then closed it and locked the door. He too then disappeared inside the same bar.

“How many tracking devices have you got with you?” I asked Richard.

“Three,” he replied, “but the best quality bugs for long range tracking are the two currently attached to bottom of the speedboat.”

“Do we still need them on the speedboat?” asked George who had now joined us.

“I wouldn’t have thought so,” I replied.

“Helena, what’re your thoughts on the subject. Keep them on the boat or get them back and use them on the cars?”

“Cars, definitely,” she replied.

“Leave it to us,” said George as he and Colin disappeared into the darkness heading down to the moored speedboat.

They were both back inside four minutes.

“All done,” said Colin, “one bug now firmly on the underside of each car.”

“Can you follow them on your iPad from now on Richard?” asked Helena.

“Yes,” he replied, “no problem as long as I am within eight miles of them, or ten at a push. I should get a good signal providing they don’t split up and head in different directions. However, I can deal with that once we’re back on the plane. I’ve got a second iPad and I’ll allocate a bug to each tablet.”

“In that case can I suggest we leave straight away,” said Helena.

“We’re a bit obvious sitting out here, and if we stay much longer we’ll be spotted. The Gulfstream is well within Richard’s eight-mile range, and we should be able to follow them easily enough from there.”

We got into both cars, quietly closed the doors, started them up and headed back to the plane.

We took it in turns to cat-nap while two of us sat glued to the two screens waiting for any movement. There was nothing for nearly two hours when Jo suddenly yelled.

"One of the cars is moving folks."

Hearing Jo's yell, we all jumped up and raced back to the two cars to follow the bugs. Jo was following the BMW on one iPad and she sat in the front seat of George's car, and Richard was following the Land Cruiser on the second iPad from the front seat of my car.

"The Toyota's on the move as well," said Richard, and at that moment, both cars were heading in the same direction. They stuck together and drove for over an hour covering virtually the entire length of Crete, eventually pulling into the short stay car park area of Heraklion airport. One man got out of the Toyota and headed for departures, with the rest of them locking their two vehicles, after which they headed for the bar in the airport. I recognized the man heading for departures as the boss.

"Try and see where he's going, can you please?" asked Helena of George and Jo. "If the others head off, we'll leave Colin here with the car, and you can catch us up later."

Jo was back five minutes later.

"He's just checked in for the early morning flight to Lisbon," said Jo. "George is still watching him. What do you want us to do?"

"Jump in the car for a minute Jo," replied Helena, which she did.

"Look, you guys have seen these characters earlier, and you all agree, the man getting the flight to Lisbon is their boss. Correct?"

Colin and I both nodded our agreement. Richard hadn't seen him.

"Any idea what time his flight arrives in Lisbon Jo?" asked Helena.

"No, but I can go and find out."

"Hold on a minute Jo," responded Helena. "My feeling is that we're not going to learn anything new or of any great importance by staying here on Crete. They obviously have a team here who do conversion work on stolen yachts, and from what you all tell me that man-made cave didn't just appear here overnight. No, there's a lot of planning gone into all this. My gut feeling is to shut up shop here in Crete, all get on the Gulfstream and head for Lisbon ensuring we get there before their boss, and then follow him when he lands. What do you think?"

"Makes perfect sense to me," said Sam.

"Likewise," I agreed.

"OK then Jo," said Helena. "Can you go and find out what time his flight is due to land in Lisbon, then collect George and we'll all head back to the plane. We'll wait here till you and George get back. Colin, can you please go and retrieve Richard's two bugs from their cars. We don't want them being found by some mechanic."

Jo disappeared back into the airport, and then reappeared five minutes later with George.

"His flight lands at 08:15 a.m.," said Jo. "After he'd checked his bag in, he then went and joined the others in the bar."

Colin returned to the car clasping two grime covered bugs in his hand, which he then passed to Richard. Helena then suggested we all get back to the Gulfstream and make our way to Lisbon as fast as possible. We could have a rest once we got there – if we had time.

The 'boss's' flight did in fact land ten minutes early, but we'd been in Lisbon a couple of hours by then and we'd all had time to freshen up, change our clothes and eat some breakfast. Richard had fixed us all up with tiny two-way radio communication links, so that everybody could hear and speak to everybody else, and nobody noticed a thing as we all looked as if we were listening to music or using a hands free mobile phone. Helena had instructed us all to keep quiet unless it was necessary, in other words, no idle chit chat. We split up into three pairs, Sam and myself, Richard and Helena, and finally Jo and George, with Colin hovering on his own at the newspaper stand. We waited in three different areas of the arrivals hall. Whichever way 'the boss' went, we had him covered.

About twenty minutes after his plane landed he emerged from the customs area towing his black flight case and entered the main arrivals hall. He turned sharp right and then Colin's voice came over the radio.

"He's heading in my direction folks. Looks like the railway station."

"Try and get immediately behind him Colin if you can," urged Helena. "Try and find out where he's going. The rest of us will all join you on the platform."

We all made our way speedily to the ticket office where Colin had already bought seven single tickets, one for each of us. Our target, 'the boss', had already gone onto the platform.

"No rush," said Colin looking at his watch. "The train doesn't leave for another twelve minutes."

"Split up into your pairs on the train," commanded Helena.

"Please don't in any way acknowledge each other, and make sure at least one of each pair can see him at all times."

"So, Colin," asked Sam, "Where are we all going?"

"Faro," came Colin's single word reply.

Chapter Fifteen

We all boarded the same carriage on the fast train to Faro stopping at just six other stations en route. George and Jo sat with their back to the front of the train, with 'the boss' sitting the other side of the central aisle, but he was facing the front. Helena and Richard sat immediately behind George and Jo and they could see the top of 'the boss's head, so they would know if he moved. Sam and I sat two rows behind 'the boss' and Colin sat facing us. Richard's two-way communications system was still in use amongst us all with one microphone and one earpiece per pair. Helena's instructions had been very strict in that we were not to look at him or stare at him for any reason, and that if our target travelled all the way to Faro, then we should stay in our pairs and casually form a standard surveillance box around him. However, if he got up and left the train at an earlier station, then only Colin, Sam and I were to follow him. He seemed to be totally unaware that he was under the watchful gaze of seven pairs of eyes, and he casually read through a Portuguese newspaper, flicked through a magazine, and drank a coffee brought round by the lady on the trolley service. When he wasn't doing any of those he simply gazed out of the window or dozed off. Our plan for an early exit from the train wasn't needed, as he stayed firmly in his seat to the end of the line.

When we pulled into Faro, George and Jo made sure they got off the train in front of him, and quickly walked out of the station to take up position at either the front or the back of the box, depending which way our target moved. George and Jo turned right out of Faro station and slowly headed in the direction of the small marina. Colin headed into the newsagents and bought a newspaper, ensuring our man was well in front of him. The remaining four of us took up our respective positions in order to complete the box around him. Our man, 'the boss', also turned right and made his way towards the marina, and the excellent bar restaurant overlooking all the small boats. Once he arrived, he sat at one of the outside tables and ordered a bottle of Sagres, the local beer, and a brandy.

Helena, out of sight from our man beckoned Colin over to her.

"The second, he leaves," she said, "grab his brandy glass and the empty beer bottle, and put them in separate evidence bags. I assume you've got some on you?"

"Of course," said Colin as he replied.

"I want to see if we've got this character's fingerprints on file," she continued.

"Will do boss," replied Colin.

Our man sat at his table for about ten minutes, then got up and left, leaving the money for his drinks on the table. Before the waiter could get anywhere near the empties, Colin, now wearing a pair of latex gloves, had snatched the glass and the empty bottle off of the table and disappeared with them both. The waiter didn't seem in the least bit bothered, after all, he'd still got the money. Helena had asked Sam and me to tail him if he walked, but the minute we'd arrived at the marina bar Helena had been on the phone to our old police friend and colleague Inspector Paulo Cabrita of the Portuguese GNR. She asked him if it might be possible for an unmarked car to pick her and Richard up, and then follow our man if he got a cab or was collected. Paulo had arrived himself in his own private car about five minutes before our man left.

As it happened, our man took a leisurely stroll into the center of Faro, and let himself into a smart looking apartment block with his front door key. The block had four separate doors, and our man had gone into the third one. Sam and I had followed him all the way as instructed, and we made a note of his address when we got there, then, as also instructed by Helena, we all got taxis back to my villa, apart from Helena who arrived with Paulo. The takeaway food man arrived fifteen minutes later, and then the eight of us all sat around the dining table stuffing our faces with copious amounts of chicken & chips and cold beer, whilst we all chipped in on what we'd learnt so far, therefore bringing Paulo up to date now that the investigation had at last landed in his territory.

"Is it possible Paulo," began Helena. "For you to put our suspect under some discreet surveillance for the next few days? I'd like to know where he goes, whom he meets with etc."

"No problem," replied Paulo. "I'll organize that immediately. Having seen your man in question briefly at the marina bar, I can't say that I recognized him, but we should have fingerprint ID back soon, and hopefully a name. As you requested, I also sent the same set of fingerprints to Kurt and asked him to search the Interpol files as he may well be clean in Portugal."

"I wouldn't mind betting he's on a file somewhere," I said, and as I spoke Helena's mobile phone pinged to indicate she'd received an email.

"You're right Michael," she said

"Our man is on the Interpol database. Kurt put his fingerprints through the Interpol search engine and got a hit. He is a forty-six-year-old Portuguese man named Alexio Ribeiro. Portuguese father and a Greek mother."

"Aha," said Jo, "The Greek connection."

"He got involved with some petty smuggling in Greece when he was in his early twenties," continued Helena.

"But as far as we know he's kept his nose clean ever since."

"As far as we know?" I mused aloud.

"Oh, you'll like this," she said. "Although his father was Portuguese, he was born on the Greek island of Crete where most of his mother's family still live and work."

"I wouldn't mind betting the family business is now upmarket boat conversions," said George with a laugh in his voice.

"He's more than likely the link man between the theft of yachts, converting them, and then possibly selling them on."

"Let's not get ahead of ourselves," warned Helena. "All we know for sure about Mr. Ribeiro is that he oversaw hiding the 'Nefertiti' in the cave in order to get the camouflage work done. We don't know for sure what else he's involved with, and he may not even know the forger, or for that matter he may not even know who the forger is. No, I think we have to follow Mr. Ribeiro over the next few days and see where he leads us."

"What can I do, officially and unofficially?" asked Paulo.

"To be honest Paulo, just follow him. See where he goes and what he does. I assume your men can be suitably discreet?" asked Helena.

"No problem, my own team is very good. I'll go and brief them now and I'll keep in touch with you by phone or email. Many thanks for the chicken & chips and the beer Michael," Paulo yelled back as he was leaving the dining room.

"Oh please. Don't thank me," I shouted back. "Interpol will be paying."

"Mean old skinflint," said Sam, giving me a dirty look. Then we all laughed.

Chapter Sixteen

Paulo's men, well I say men, there were four men and two women in the team actually; anyway as I was saying, they followed Alexio Ribeiro for the next two days and confirmed that all he'd done was go to the charter boat service he ran from the marina at Vilamoura. He'd get there ready to start work at ten in the morning, close for lunch between one and three during which he'd also have a brief siesta, and then he'd open up again and work until he left in the evening, usually around seven o'clock, at which point he drove home. At least that's all he did on the first two days. On day three however he did exactly the same, but instead of going home he got in his car and drove to a small town between Faro and Almancil called São Lourenço. Behind the town's large Catholic Church is a lightly wooded area with half a dozen small warehouses set back amongst the trees. Ribeiro drove up to the end one of these white-colored warehouses and went inside. He didn't come out again for over two hours.

When he eventually left the warehouse, one of the surveillance team's cars followed him home, while the other car, on Paulo's instructions, waited until everybody else left in the warehouse also went home. Just after midnight, the last person out locked up. The surveillance team telephoned Paulo who had phoned Helena earlier and got all of us together about half a mile from the warehouse where we now all sat and waited in our cars. Once we got the all clear signal from Paulo's team, we drove a bit closer, and then George, Colin and Jo, all dressed in their best black outfits, did their covert operation thing and very carefully broke into the warehouse. Paulo said he was more than happy to leave the covert stuff to Interpol and he really didn't want to get involved at this stage as he hadn't reported any of this to his big bosses in Lisbon. Having got inside George, Colin and Jo then photographed everything in sight, took loads of fingerprints from numerous bits of machinery, being very careful to clean off the fingerprint dust as they went, they copied various documents on their own portable photocopier they'd taken in with them, and then very carefully ensuring there was no trace of their visit, they carefully locked up behind themselves and left.

We all went back to my villa where Sam and I served drinks to everyone while Richard downloaded all the photographs and fingerprints onto his laptops. Fifteen minutes later we sat down to watch the show as Richard displayed the results on the one white wall in the lounge, once of course we'd ensured all the curtains were closed. As he showed us the pictures, Richard spoke:

"Ladies and gentlemen, you are without doubt looking at an ultra-high quality, top of the range print shop whose sole purpose in life at the moment appears to be printing vast amounts of counterfeit euros, sterling and US dollars. The printing machines, the industrial guillotines, the poly wrap machines etc. are all top professional gear, and from the close-up photographs of the fifty and one hundred euro notes George took, it seems to my untrained eye that the quality is bloody excellent."

"Does this mean we've cracked it then and found the Faro Forger?" asked Sam.

"I very much doubt it," replied Helena.

"The first thing I did on returning to the villa," said Richard again, "was to upload the fingerprints and send them straight to Kurt. We've got some preliminary response, but from what he is saying, these all appear to be grunts and lowly print workers. No bosses I'm afraid, and certainly no Faro Forger."

"Richard is right. I'm sure," said Helena, smiling at him.

"This is good progress, and at least we now know the location of one of their print shops. But who's to say there aren't five more print shops churning out counterfeit in five other countries. Until we find the forger, we won't find the bosses, and although we set out looking for the Faro Forger, what we actually want in reality are the people he works for."

"I suppose for all we know," I surmised aloud, "the Faro Forger may have never set foot in Portugal at all, but in fact engraves all his printing plates on some remote island of the coast of Thailand, and then he simply ships them to Faro for the printing process."

“Exactly,” responded Helena. “Look, we’ve made excellent progress today and we have some really good leads. It’s now one thirty in the morning and I’m shattered. Can I suggest that we all get some sleep, and if it’s all right with Michael, we’ll meet back here for one of your famous full English working breakfasts at ten o’clock?”

It was fine by me, and I said so.

Chapter Seventeen

Two fried eggs, sunny side up of course, two rashers of lean back bacon, two pork sausages, a small pile of baked beans, two grilled half tomatoes, four small hash browns, two slices of fried bread, and all supplied with HP Brown sauce. That was what Helena referred to as my famous full English working breakfast. Everyone was sitting round the table by 9:15 a.m., and the breakfasts appeared on the table promptly at ten o'clock. By 10:30 a.m. I have to say, there wasn't a speck of leftovers on anybody's plate. I'm not a great cook by anyone's definition, but I can do a pretty mean full English. Both during and after breakfast, we chatted about anything and everything that wasn't to do with the case; football, weather (which we discussed naturally, being English), wild fires that had broken out in the north of Portugal, the sorry state of the pound against the euro and the dollar – as I said, anything and everything. Helena then made an announcement.

"OK everyone. Back to work I'm afraid. Just to let you know, I received an urgent telephone call from Kurt at some unearthly hour this morning."

"It was nearly 3:00 a.m. for goodness sake," said Richard, without thinking.

"And how on earth would you know what time Helena received a phone call in her bedroom, young man ?" queried Sam with a smile on her face. Both Richard and Helena had the good grace to blush.

"Sorry," mouthed Richard to Helena, who just smiled back at him.

"As I was saying," she continued. "Kurt has been in Greenwich working with both Stephen and Paul on certain aspects which relate directly to the UK, and while he was there he received all the information we'd gathered in both Crete and Faro over the last few days. Kurt has had Interpol's people in

Amsterdam as well as some of Stephen's people following up leads all over the place. Apparently, he now has some news which he wanted to tell us about himself, so he, along with Stephen and Paul are on the early flight from Gatwick and they should all be with us in about half an hour. Paulo is also on his way here, and Kurt said they'll fill us in on everything they've discovered when they get here. Richard, can you set up your laptops and the screen here in the lounge please, and Michael, can we find some more chairs please?"

I disappeared upstairs with George and Colin and we returned with four reasonably comfortable chairs taken from various bedrooms. I did some quick Math based on everyone that was going to be at the meeting. Sam and I were two, Helena and Richard made four, George, Colin and Jo, made it seven, Kurt, Stephen and Paul would bring it up to ten, and Paulo would make it eleven. We just about had enough chairs and also had just about enough room in the lounge. While we were sorting chairs, Sam and Jo put two kettles on and the coffee machine. Fortunately, we had about forty mugs in the villa, so that wasn't a problem.

Paulo arrived first, with Kurt, Stephen and Paul about five minutes behind him. There were all the usual greetings and then everyone sat down and Kurt took over the meeting.

"Firstly," he began, "thank you Michael for allowing us to use your home for this, it is greatly appreciated. We've been working very hard over the last twelve hours and a lot of information has come to light as a direct result of your sleuthing in Canada, Crete and Faro.

"In cooperation with Paulo, we put a twenty-four-hour tail on our Cretan friend, Mr. Alexio Ribeiro, opened and then resealed his post, and tapped his phones. He has a land line in the house and a mobile which we managed to tap into with a warrant instructing the Portuguese service provider to cooperate with us, or else. They cooperated. We then recorded all his conversations, during which we discovered he reports to a boss far higher up the food chain."

"Is that someone here in Faro, or back in Crete?" I asked.

"Neither," said Kurt. "Paul, perhaps you should take over at this point."

“Sure,” said Paul. “Mr. Ribeiro made a telephone call in the early hours reporting that they had the package safely hidden away and the transformation should be finished in approximately two months. He then asked if there were any further instructions at this time, and the man on the other end of the phone said he needed to think about it and would ring him back. We assume the package hidden away is the ‘Nefertiti’ hidden in the cave.”

“So, if he wasn’t ringing Faro or Crete, where was he telephoning?” I asked again.

“Abu Dhabi,” replied Stephen.

“Abu Dhabi!” exclaimed about four people at the same time.

“To cut a long story short,” said Paul, “it looks like this entire operation is being run by two brothers of an excruciatingly rich family who are based in Abu Dhabi.”

“That’s a city in Dubai, isn’t it?” asked Jo.

“Oh no,” replied Paul. “And don’t ever let anyone from Abu Dhabi hear you say that. Look, I’m sorry to ask this and I don’t mean to be rude, but how much do you folks all know about the Middle East?” he asked as a general question.

“I’ve flown in and out of Dubai’s airport a few times,” said George. “But other than that, I know nothing about the area.”

“OK,” said Paul. “In that case I’ll try and fill you in as best I can, as I think this is where you’re all going to be heading next.”

“I thought we were after the Faro Forger,” said Sam.

“We are,” replied Paul, “but we believe his bosses operate out of Abu Dhabi. Let me explain a bit of general information about the Middle East. It’s all fairly important if you want to understand what’s going on, so please make notes if you think it will help.”

Most of us had pens and notepads in front of us anyway, but Paulo went digging in his briefcase while Colin shot up to the bedroom he was sharing with George and grabbed a pad and a pen, and then came running back down, taking the stairs two at a time.

“The Middle East as we call it,” started Paul, “is dominated by three countries as far as land area is concerned. Those three are Saudi Arabia, Iraq and Iran, but as far as we are aware, none of them has anything to do with any of this. No, the countries we are interested in are the UAE and Oman. Now the UAE stands for the United Arab Emirates.”

"What exactly is an Emirate?" asked Sam. "Is it different to a country?"

"An Emirate is simply a political territory ruled by a dynastic Islamic monarch known as an Emir."

"Sorry," Sam said. "Can you repeat that please Paul? Slowly, and in English."

"OK. A political territory, like a country for example, that is ruled by a dynastic Islamic monarch, i.e. a Moslem King or Emir as they call it, and power it is passed down through the family or dynasty."

"And the United Arab Emirates is a group of them?" continued Sam. "Sorry if I seem a bit stupid, but I'd like to know."

"Although I've flown into Dubai several times," said Jo, "I'm like you Sam, I know very little about the various countries or Emirates at all."

"OK everyone, I guess there are going to be lots of questions, which is fair enough, but can I then request that you just let me go through this, and if you've still got questions write them down on your pads, and I'll deal with them if I can at the end."

Everyone thought this was a good idea and kept quiet so that Paul could get on with it.

"The UAE, or United Arab Emirates is what is called a federal absolute monarchy, and it is located at the southeast end of the Arabian Peninsula on the Persian Gulf. Its neighbors are Oman to the east and Saudi Arabia to the south, and it shares maritime borders with Qatar to the west and Iran to the north. The UAE's population is roughly ten million, of which only one and a half million are actually Emirati citizens, and the other eight and a half million are expatriates of numerous other nationalities.

The UAE is a federation of seven emirates, and was originally established on the second of December 1971, after Harold Wilson's British government decided it couldn't afford to protect the Sheikdoms any more. There are now seven emirates in the UAE, the original six which are Abu Dhabi, Ajman, Dubai, Fujairah, Sharjah and Umm Al-Quwain, with the seventh Ras Al-Khaimah joining the UAE the following year. Each emirate is governed by an absolute monarch or Emir, and together those seven Sheiks form the Federal Supreme

Council, one of whom is selected as the President of the United Arab Emirates.

Islam is the official religion, and Arabic is the official language, although English is the language of business and education, particularly in the capital Abu Dhabi and Dubai."

"I thought Dubai was the capital?" I queried.

"A common mistake Michael," replied Paul. "Abu Dhabi is not only the capital, it covers an area of nearly twenty-six thousand square miles, which is over eighty five percent of the UAE's total land area. Don't ever say Dubai is the capital if you're in the UAE."

"I assume their wealth has come from oil?" asked Colin.

"The UAE's incredible wealth actually comes from two plentiful natural products. Its oil reserves are the seventh largest in the world, while its natural gas reserves are the seventeenth largest in the world. The first President of the UAE was Sheikh Zayed, the ruler of Abu Dhabi and he was a very wise man, much loved by his people. He oversaw and controlled all the development of the Emirates, and he cleverly steered oil revenues into healthcare, education and infrastructure."

"Isn't there a lot of crime there?" asked Jo. "Sharia law and all that?"

"If you have ever been to the UAE and walked around the streets, you will know it feels incredibly safe, and it is one of the few countries in the world where women can feel safe walking around at night. I remember talking to an English friend of mine who lives and works in Dubai, and he has had an apartment in Dubai for over ten years now, and he told me he hasn't bothered to lock his front door now for over seven years."

"But isn't this the part of the world where ISIS come from?" asked Paulo. "Please excuse my ignorance, I've never been to the Middle East, and I can only go by what I see on the TV. Surely they've have been terrorizing the west for years now."

"No, I totally understand Paulo. If you don't know about something from personal experience, you can only go by what you're told or what you see and hear from the media. Yes, the UAE is a Muslim country, but as far as religion is concerned, the UAE prides itself on being a very tolerant society in which no religions are persecuted. The population is roughly, and I do mean roughly, seventy-five percent Muslim, fifteen percent

Hindu due to the vast amount of migrant Indian workers, and ten percent Christian. Ninety-nine percent of the world's Muslims are peace loving and abhor everything ISIS stands for. As far as ISIS is concerned, the UAE helped the USA launch its first air offensive against Islamic State targets in Syria."

"Sorry Paul," said Paulo, "I had no idea."

"No problem," said Paul. "I only know a lot of this because I researched it for this meeting, and from my own personal experience. I've been to Dubai and Abu Dhabi several times over the last five years on various holidays and to visit my mate who has a fabulous apartment overlooking Dubai marina. I could quite happily live there."

"So, does the UAE have a big army, navy and air force of its own?" I asked.

"Not massive," answered Paul. "Although initially small in number, the UAE's armed forces have grown significantly over the last few years, and they are now equipped with some of the most modern weapon systems available in the world, purchased from a variety of outside countries, mainly France, the USA and ourselves in the UK. Interestingly, you'll find most of the UAE's military officers are in fact graduates of the UK's own Royal Military Academy at Sandhurst."

"OK everyone," said Stephen. "Thank you, Paul, for all the background information. Now as for our two brothers. Kurt, can I hand back to you please?"

"Yes of course, and can I just add my thanks as well Paul. That was really informative and very helpful. Now, as for our two brothers. Having done some research of our own, Interpol has discovered that our two brothers are Ahmed and Nudara Bukhari. We believe that that these two are in fact illegitimate sons of one of the most influential Sheiks in the UAE, but he does not admit to them being his sons or admit they are related to him in any way, and consequently he has refused to recognize them, and has totally excluded them from sharing in the family's vast wealth. As Paul said, that wealth comes from two natural sources, oil and gas, and Ahmed and Nudara rightly or wrongly feel very hard done by."

"I should say that they are far from poor," said Stephen, "as their mother is very well looked after by the Sheik, but it is nowhere near the sort of wealth they would have had access to if they had been officially recognized by their father."

"So," continued Kurt. "Our two brothers have set themselves up in all manner of illegal businesses, and decided to go about creating their own wealth, and from what we can tell they are doing very nicely. Our telephone tap showed it was Ahmed Bukhari that Alexio Ribeiro spoke to on his mobile yesterday, and it is our firm belief that Ahmed and Nudara are both the brains and the money behind all the counterfeiting, forged bank drafts, yacht thefts, car thefts etc. One of the documents Colin photocopied in the Faro Printshop was an order for a massive new Thomas De La Rue printing press, the ideal press, our experts tell us, for printing counterfeit currency. De la Rue have strict rules governing whom they do and don't sell to, and they check everything thoroughly."

"These presses can of course be used for numerous other printing purposes," said Stephen. "And the order they received, accompanied by a second document issued by the purchasing government authorizing the transaction, stated that the press was required for printing government stationery and publicity material in the emerging economies of Estonia, one of the old Soviet republics. The press was duly delivered to Tallinn."

"However," continued Kurt taking over again, "The printing press wasn't even taken out of its crate before being put straight into the hold of a cargo ship sailing from Tallinn, through the Baltic, down through the North Sea to eventually be offloaded in Lisbon, where it was finally transported to Faro on the back of an articulated truck. De La Rue we are sure were, and for that matter probably still are, totally unaware of what their press was going to be used for, and after all they had an official government purchase order from Estonia. Except of course that too had been forged. That order had an authorizing signature on the bottom of it that our handwriting experts tell us was signed by Nudara Bukhari."

"At a very rough calculation," said Paul, "and based only on what we know about for sure, we estimate that the Bukharis have so far netted well in excess of three hundred and fifty million pounds. However, I'm afraid that is nothing when you look at their ambition, which is to get as much money into their own bank account as they feel they have been deprived of by their own father denying their existence."

"Now, ninety percent of this is not provable at this stage," said Stephen. "It's that old police favorite – lack of evidence – and that's where you all come in. We would like all seven of you to go to Abu Dhabi and Dubai. The Bukhari brothers appear to have premises in both Emirates, as well as having several warehouses located on the east coast of Oman, just south of the capital, Muscat."

"Is that another Emirate?" asked Jo.

"No," said Paul. "Oman has one of the only two, true Sultans left in the world. The other is the Sultan of Brunei. What you have to understand is that Oman is an absolute monarchy, and that means the Sultan's rule is total. If the Sultan of Oman can't sleep, wakes up at three o'clock in the morning and decides every public telephone box should be painted purple by midday, it will happen. He has to consult nobody. As I said, Oman is an absolute monarchy. Fortunately, the current Sultan is much loved by all Omanis and he is now the longest serving ruler in the Middle East."

"So, what you are telling us, Paul," said Sam, "is whether we go to Abu Dhabi, Dubai or Oman, we'll definitely be safe?"

"Exactly."

"Now what we need you to do when you get there," said Kurt taking over again, "is to visit the offices of the Bukharis in Abu Dhabi and their apartment in Dubai, and try and see what they're up to there. I've already briefed Helena on a few ideas that should get you through their door. Also see if you can sneak a look into their warehouses which are located just outside Muscat in Oman. Richard will have map coordinates for everywhere you need to visit, and we will issue you all with the necessary visas and paperwork before you leave. Any questions at this stage?"

We all looked blankly at each other, and then I said:

"I assume if we think of a question we can ask you?"

"Yes of course," replied Kurt. "But please put all your questions through Helena. She'll be in total charge again, and what she says goes. OK?"

We all nodded our agreement, and five minutes later the meeting broke up.

Chapter Eighteen

We set off in the Gulfstream the following morning with George at the controls, Colin in the co-pilot's seat and Jo serving coffee to everyone. Sam, Helena, Richard and myself sat in the comfortable leather chairs discussing the various ideas for getting to the Bukharis that Kurt had given Helena the day before. Jo joined us once we all had a coffee.

"Helena," said Sam. "Kurt said yesterday that he'd given you a few ideas about how to get through the door of the Bukhari's office and apartment. Can you enlighten us, please?"

"Of course. Kurt's idea is very simple. We break in, in the middle of the night and copy everything we can find in drawers, files, on computers etc."

"Well I can't speak for anybody else," I began. "But I'm one hundred percent sure that is not an area of expertise I possess."

"I'm sorry Helena," said Jo. "I know George, Colin and myself have all been trained in covert operations, but that's not something we ever covered in great depth, and I for one wouldn't be keen on trying to steal documents from a country where they chop off your hands if you're caught thieving."

"That's Saudi, not the UAE," I replied. "Nobody will chop your hands off even if you did get caught, but I do take your point Jo."

"That's why," said Helena interrupting our flow, "we're stopping in Rome en route to the UAE. We're picking up another team member who does have the required expertise. We're picking up your good friend Martin Smith who flew to Rome yesterday from Johannesburg."

"Who's Martin Smith?" asked Jo.

"That's not his real name," I replied. "By the way Helena, what is it?"

"I could tell you Michael," smiled Helena, and then we all said together:

"But then I'd have to kill you!"

We all laughed, and then Helena continued:

"Actually, Martin is his real name, we just changed the surname. Martin is South Africa's foremost cat burglar, covert operative, whatever you want to call him, and is definitely in the world's top ten of burglars. He has been working exclusively for Kurt and Interpol for the last six years, and last year he worked with Michael and Sam on the previous job they were doing for us in the Bahamas. He's a great guy and knows what he's doing. If we all follow his instructions to the letter we'll be fine."

We landed in Rome and taxied to a private hanger where the Gulfstream was refueled. A few minutes later, a black BMW drove into the hanger, and Martin got out of the car. Sam and I went down the steps to meet him.

"Sam, Michael, how the hell are you both?" he asked.

"It's great to see you again, and hi to you too Helena," who had just appeared at the top of the plane's steps.

Everybody got off the plane and stretched their legs while Colin supervised the loading of all six of Martin's silver flight cases and his one suitcase into the Gulfstream's hold. After all the introductions had been completed we all boarded the plane again, and sat in the main lounge area of the fuselage where Helena briefed Martin and the rest of us on Kurt's plan.

"OK everyone. Kurt's idea is basically very simple. As I said previously, the idea is to break in to their apartment in the middle of the night and copy everything we can find in drawers, files, on computers etc. Now there are various problems that will make this more difficult than a lot of other burglaries, and that's why Kurt has sent us Martin. Problem one is that our two targets live in the Burj Khalifa."

"That's the seven-star hotel shaped like a ship's sail, isn't it?" asked Richard.

"No, sorry Richard," I replied. "The hotel you're thinking of is the Burj Al Arab. The Burj Khalifa is the tallest building in the world, and so I assume Martin you won't be climbing down from the roof?" I jokingly asked.

"Too bloody right I won't," he replied laughing. "Kurt told me where to find the brothers' apartment, and so I've been doing some homework on the building. One good thing about it is that because it is the tallest building in the world it attracts a hell of a

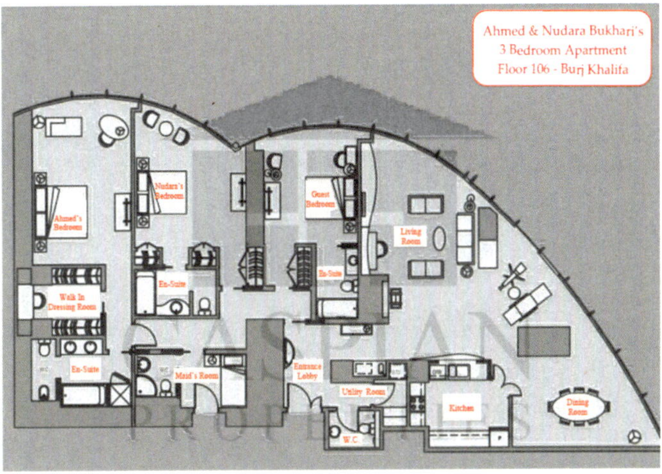

Floor Plan of Ahmed and Nudara Bukhari's Apartment

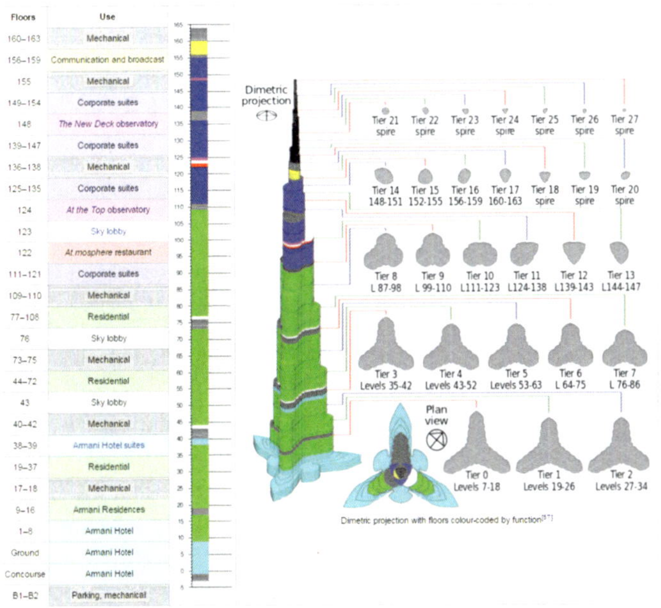

Floor Plan of the Burg Khalifa, Dubai

The Burg Khalifa in Dubai, the tallest building in the world

lot of tourists, and access to the observation deck on the hundred and twenty fourth floor is easy as it's open to the public all day from 9:30 a.m.'

Is it all apartments, offices or what?' asked Sam.

"It's very mixed," replied Martin. "The lower floors from the concourse up to the sixteenth floor all belong to the Armani Hotel or the Armani Residences. There're then a couple of floors given over to the building's mechanical needs, and then floors nineteen to thirty-nine are all residential again."

"So, no offices," I asked.

"Not on the lower levels, but there are what's described as corporate suites on several of the upper floors, and a lot of those are glorified offices for big companies."

"So where do we find Ahmed and Nudara Bukhari?" asked George.

"They have a large residential suite on the one hundred and sixth floor, which is great from our point of view as there are another couple of floors above them given over to more mechanical equipment on levels one hundred and nine and one ten."

"Sorry Martin," asked Sam. "But why is that good?'

"I think I can hopefully answer that one," smiled George. "At some point in its life, all mechanical equipment either breaks down or needs servicing, and that requires men in overalls to come and repair it. We can easily become men in overalls. Yes or no Martin?"

"Spot on George. We will simply go in one morning dressed in our very best 'Farnek Services LLC' overalls; they are the company that have the maintenance contract for the building by the way. We'll go up to the one hundred and ninth floor and find a secluded area where we can safely hide all the equipment we'll need later for the break in. We'll then leave the building half an hour later. We'll have to check in and check out, but I'm sure providing the number of people in and out match we'll be fine."

"So basically, we just walk in and dump everything we need for later use?" said George. "And then walk out?"

"Exactly. Now the last tour of the day goes up to the observatory, which is on the hundred and twenty fourth floor, at five thirty, and everyone has to be out by six. We'll go up in that last tour group and then discreetly make our way down the stairs to the hundred and ninth where we'll hide out amongst the machinery until two in the morning."

"Nobody will try and stop us using the stairs?' asked Colin.

"They may do," replied Martin, "but I doubt it. It will be very long and extremely tedious hiding amongst the machinery for hours on end, but it's the only way of doing it. We go into the apartment at 2:30 a.m. and copy everything in sight. If the Bukhari brothers are there, they'll be drugged with a harmless gas that will give us a couple of hours to search everywhere, and then we'll make sure we're out and back in our hidey hole by 5:00 a.m. where we leave anything we've copied for the time being. We can't leave straight away as nobody is supposed to be working that early. At nine o'clock we make our way out in our overalls having collected all our equipment and the copies of everything which we'll have stashed away earlier. Hopefully we simply walk out."

"You make it sound so easy Martin," said Sam, "but there must be risks?"

"Of course, there are risks, but the more professional we are about the break in, the less chance there is of anything going wrong."

"You kept referring to 'we' during the briefing," I said. "Who's breaking in with you?"

"You are Michael, because I've worked with you before and I know that after the Bahamas incident, you'll do exactly what you're told and only what you're told, plus George and Colin because Kurt assures me they've been trained in covert work."

"What about the rest of us," asked Sam?

"I'll need Richard and Helena to be in constant communication with me," replied Martin. "Particularly during the break in phase, and Sam and Jo, you will be acting as lookouts at every stage of the operation. Whenever we're on the inside, you'll all be on the outside keeping a sharp lookout for any unwelcome visitors, both outside their apartment or on the mechanical floors. I also need you on the radio giving warnings if necessary. To avoid constant chatter, I want just one radio set with each group. That will be me in the break-in team, Helena in overall control and making final decisions and Sam on the lookout team. I assume you have enough powerful long range comm's gear to handle that Richard?"

"Yes, no problem," he replied.

"Where the hell do we get four sets of 'Farnek Services' overalls?" I asked.

"They're already in the hold of the Gulfstream," replied Martin. "Kurt had four sets made up before I left this morning and he put them in one of the silver cases. I'm afraid they're one size fits all, but for what we need they'll be fine. As I said earlier, we have to be professional about every aspect of this. There's no rush, and we only do the break in once we've established and confirmed everything we need to know in advance."

"Apart from the Bukhari's apartment in the Burj Khalifa, Kurt said they also have offices in Abu Dhabi and warehouses in Oman. Will we be visiting them as well?" I asked.

"God, they'll be sick of us by the time we've done all that," said Jo.

"No, they won't, Jo," said Martin. "As they'll never even know they've been visited if we all do our jobs properly, but I do know what you mean," he laughed.

"Kurt has given Martin complete authority over the burglary stages," said Helena.

"So please, if Martin asks you to do something, don't check with me. Just do it. OK, George?"

She said, "In the words of the truly wonderfully delicious Mr. Kenneth More, can we please reach for the sky?"

"Who the hell's Kenneth More?" whispered Richard in my ear.

"Oh, he was an actor in an old black and white film about an RAF pilot named Douglas Bader who lost his both his legs, but still carried on flying spitfires throughout the Second World War. You know if you are going to go out with Helena you're going to have to swat up on your films Richard. You know how much she loves her old movies."

"I know, but there's so damned many of them," he laughed.

George had started the Gulfstream's twin jets, and we gently moved out of the hanger, taxied to the end of the runway and then as Helena had said – we reached for the sky.

The flight to Dubai International took us about five hours, and once we'd landed and put the Gulfstream in its prearranged hanger, there were be two BMW 7 series hire cars waiting for us. They don't do cheap cars in Dubai! Once we'd landed and taxied into the hanger, we loaded all our own suit cases and bags, plus of course Richard's and Martin's silver flight cases in the two BMW's boots. A customs official came into the hanger and gave us a form to say that everything had been checked and cleared by customs, even though they hadn't looked in either car or in the Gulfstream. Apparently, Kurt had been on the phone to them, and that was enough. Kurt had worked with UAE customs previously.

In order to pass the time on the flight, I had been reading a brochure originally produced by the developers about the Burj Khalifa, jam packed with fascinating facts. According to the glossy brochure, the Burj Khalifa is 2,717 feet high, and in order to assist people either going up or down the building, it contains a total of 57 elevators, 8 escalators and 2,909 stairs. The 304-room Armani Hotel occupies 15 of the lower 39 floors, and the two sky lobbies on the 43rd and 76th floors both house swimming pools. Floors 44 through to 108 have 900 private residential apartments, which, according to the developer, completely sold out within eight hours of being on the market. Corporate offices and suites fill most of the remaining floors, except for the 122nd, 123rd and 124th floors where the Atmosphere restaurant, the sky lobby and an indoor / outdoor observation deck are located respectively. The building is in fact so tall that on the higher floors, people can still see the sun for a couple of minutes after it has already set on the ground. This had apparently led Muslim clerics in Dubai to rule that those people living above the 80th floor of the building should wait for an additional two minutes before breaking their Ramadan fast, and those above the 150th floor should wait for an additional 3 minutes. As well as the glossy brochure I'd been reading, Martin had also managed to acquire through Kurt, a detailed copy of the floor plan of the Burj Khalifa, and in particular a detailed floor plan of the apartment we would eventually be breaking into. All very helpful information.

We drove the two BMWs to our hotel, the Grand Hyatt, parked well out of the sun in the hotel's underground car park where we unloaded everything, and then took over a couple of lifts in order to get all the various bags and cases up to our rooms. Sam and I were sharing a small suite which was doubling up as our conference room for the operation. Helena and Richard who were now very obviously a couple had a double room, George and Colin were sharing a twin room, and both Jo and Martin had singles, although Martin did volunteer to share with Jo, but purely to help keep the cost down he claimed. Everyone just smiled. Our five rooms were, as requested, all in a row, with interconnecting doors, and all on the top floor of the hotel. We felt we'd get a decent amount of privacy for our various comings and goings if we were out of sight of most other guests. We all got showered and changed into fresh clothes and we then picked up a couple of taxis from the hotel to the entrance to the Burj Khalifa, which is located inside the Dubai mall, the biggest shopping mall in the world. At Martin's suggestion, we'd decided to have a look at what we were going to be facing straight away.

We bought eight tickets for the viewing deck on the hundred and twenty fourth floor, and then joined the queues of people waiting for the lifts. We only waited about five minutes, and then having entered it, our lift shot to our floor incredibly fast. To be honest it didn't feel fast, but you could tell the speed by simply watching the floor numbers flash by on the illuminated panel alongside the lift operator. We hadn't been counted into the lift, at least as far as I could tell we hadn't, so that was the first good thing in our favor. We eventually emerged on the viewing deck floor and decided to wander outside to get some fresh air and admire the view, and admire it we did. I have to say; the views were absolutely breath-taking. I'd seen the Burj Khalifa in the distance on a previous brief visit when I was just passing through Dubai en route to Singapore, but this was the first time I'd been up the tower. We all got our phones out and like good tourists, started taking pictures of each other, but Martin kept moving us around to ensure what he wanted to photograph – the walls, windows, doors, alarm panels etc. were all in the background of his photographs. There were a couple of uniformed security guards wandering around the deck, but they showed no interest in us whatsoever. After all, we were just couples on holiday taking souvenir photographs, just like everybody else.

We went back inside and bought a few souvenirs. Coffee mugs, bottle openers shaped like the building, mouse mats etc. and Martin suddenly saw and immediately bought a large and very beautiful metal and clear Perspex scale model of the Burj

Khalifa that stood about three-foot-high above its base. The various souvenirs had all been wrapped and put in carrier bags, and we were ready to leave.

"I'm going to use the toilet," I quietly announced to Sam.

"I want to see if I have to come back in here or if it's possible to head off somewhere else from the loo. Can you please do the same with the women's toilets?" and I headed for the door marked 'Gentlemen' in six different languages. Sam just nodded to me and headed off for the Ladies. We were both back inside the souvenir shop three minutes later.

"That's not good Martin," I quietly whispered to him.

"Only the one door in to the loo and only one door out. You have no choice but to come back in here."

"There're three more doors over in the other corner all marked 'staff only' said Martin. "Can you, Sam, Helena and Richard please wander over there and try and get the attention of the security guard while I try and open the doors for a peek inside. I just want to see if they lead to stairs or do they just go to stockrooms for the store. The plans Kurt got me don't show these doors."

The four of us wandered over towards the security guard who was casually keeping an eye on everybody, but in a quite relaxed way.

"I'm so sorry to bother you, sir," began Sam. "Ooh, sorry, I forgot to ask, do you speak English, although if you don't speak English you won't have a clue what I'm saying will you, and I can't speak a word of Arabic to save my life, although knowing just one word wouldn't really be much use at all would it? That's not considered rude, is it?" asked Sam looking at Helena who just laughed at her.

"No, it's not rude madam," the security guard replied with a smile, "but as you can hear I do speak quite passable English."

"Ooh, smashing," Sam replied. "This shop is really wonderful as I'm sure you know, and my friends back in England simply won't believe me when I tell them all about it. So, what I'd really like is a nice photograph of the four of us, but also showing the shop in the background. None of us can take the picture as we all need to be in it, and none of us have a selfie stick. I wonder, could you please take the photograph for us?"

All the time she had been speaking, Sam had carefully turned around pointing towards the shop, and the guard had to turn away from the doors himself in order to stay with her. Richard and Helena quickly positioned themselves between the guard's back and the doors while the conversation was taking place and they now blocked his view should he suddenly turn around. While all this was going on, starting on the left Martin began to open each of the three doors in turn about six inches, glanced through the gap and then closed it. He was about to open the third door when it opened inwards and away from him, and a male staff member emerged carrying about ten boxes of 500-piece jigsaws. Needless to say, the picture on the box was the outside of the Burg Khalifa.

"I'm really sorry, madam," replied the security guard addressing Sam, "but we are not allowed to take photographs for clients. However, I'm sure if you asked another client in the store they would be only too happy to help you."

"Oh, well thank you anyway," said Sam, having received a nod from Martin that indicated he'd seen all that he needed to.

We took a few more photographs, George having seen my mouse mat decided he wanted one as well and I showed him where I'd got mine. I then saw and bought a DVD of the fountains in the lake surrounding the Burj Khalifa that apparently 'dance to music and lights' every night, like those outside the Bellagio Hotel in Las Vegas, only better! The eight of us eventually congregated together again and then went down in the lift clutching our various souvenirs. We emerged back into the mall and went for a coffee in one of the numerous bars. We found a quiet corner where we could talk.

"I have to say, that was incredibly useful," began Martin.

"The middle door goes into an office, and the right-hand door goes into a stockroom, but I managed to sneak a quick look through the left-hand door as well, and that goes straight out to a landing with stairs going both up and down."

"Do you need to check anything else while we're here?" asked Helena.

"No, I don't think so," said Martin.

"We just have to make sure that Michael, George, Colin and myself can all sneak out through that door the day we break in. You girls and Richard will have to keep the guard occupied while the four of us get through that door. Once we're through there I don't envisage any great problems."

"Any idea yet when that's likely to be?" asked George.

"Having now had a quick look around, my gut feeling is that we burgle the Bukhari's apartment tomorrow night, which means sorting out all the tools we need tonight, and overalls on in the morning chaps."

"In that case then," said Helena, "let's head back to the hotel and have a swim before our evening meal. It's too flaming hot to do much else."

Nobody argued and thirty minutes later we were in the Grand Hyatt's swimming pool.

Chapter Nineteen

That evening after our meal, we started preparing everything we would need over the following 24 hours. Richard sorted out three of his two-way communications units and ensured they all had a set of fully charged batteries, a spare set of batteries for each unit, plus a spare earpiece and microphone for each set. Martin then checked all his equipment, laid it all out, and then explained to each of us what everything did. There were radio signal jammers, alarm sensors of various descriptions, all the usual burglars' tools, master keys of every shape and size you could think of, a small silver box of electronics that could read any and all electronic passwords when held against a door, including safe doors, a small portable photocopier, two laptops loaded with apps for doing everything under the sun, plus a host of other gear. Lastly, he brought out two white aerosol cans with the name of a well-known hairspray on them. Martin then informed George and Colin that they would be using one of these each.

"These aren't full of hairspray for use on my flowing golden locks I assume," said George. "Exactly what are they full of and what do we do with them?"

"They both contain something called Neothyl," said Martin, "which is a much easier name to remember than Methylpropylether, which is its technical name. It is basically what most people would refer to as knock out gas. The four of us will be entering the Bukhari's apartment in the early hours of the morning when they should both be asleep. You two will go straight to their two bedrooms. George will take Ahmed and Colin will take Nudara. Spraying their faces with Neothyl will ensure they stay asleep until well after we've left. And to save you asking, no, they won't know anything about it, or wake up with any nasty side effects. George, you'll have one can and you use it about twenty inches above Ahmed's face. Ensure that you have a face mask on before you start so that you don't breathe any of it in yourself, and then spray it horizontally in the air letting the droplets float down and just settle on his face. He won't feel it or hear it. These are not standard aerosols and they make no noise. A three-second burst will keep him asleep for about three hours. Colin, you'll do exactly the same above Nudara's head. Michael and myself will do nothing until you return to the lounge and assure us that both brothers are out for the count and will not be walking in on us."

"OK," said Colin. "Anything else we need to go over?"

"Just a bit," said Martin, and then with us all sitting in a circle, and using the model of the Burj Khalifa he'd bought earlier sitting on the coffee table, he slowly walked us through everything that was going to happen the following day. When he'd finished, he then did it all again and asked questions of each of us in turn. If anyone got anything wrong, we had to start again. At 1:30 a.m. we all managed to score one hundred percent, and thankfully we were dismissed by Martin and went to bed.

We were all up and breakfasted by 9:00 a.m., and after dressing in our overalls, putting them over shirts and trousers, Martin, George, Colin and myself drove to the mall in one of the BMWs and parked in the massive underground car park. We had managed to pack everything we needed into just three silver-colored metal cases, and two rucksacks which George and Colin carried over their shoulders. We had located the staff entrance to the Burj Khalifa the day before, and the two security guards on duty took one look at our white overalls, complete with the 'Farnek Services' logo embroidered in orange and black, and all four of us wearing white safety helmets and goggles, and assumed we were all genuine employees and waived us through.

The goggles weren't really necessary, but wearing them helped disguise our faces. Martin was holding a clipboard with a 'Farnek Services' worksheet on it that Richard had designed and printed the night before, just in case. We caught a maintenance lift to the hundred and ninth floor, where we got out and made our way round to the various mechanical rooms. They were each full of electrical boards, hydraulic equipment, pipes and cables running everywhere, plus there were about ten different storerooms. We started at one end of the corridor and entered the various storerooms, and then in the sixth Martin immediately said:

"This'll do us nicely guys. Dump everything on the metal shelves at the back there, behind the stocks of electric cable."

There were 30 or 40 rolls of medium thick black electrical cable on the shelf, and about 20 rolls in grey. We pulled them all forward enough to create plenty of space behind them where we hid the three silver cases and our two rucksacks.

"Everybody remember where this room is," said Martin.

"We don't want to get here at two o'clock in the morning and find we've gone to the wrong room. Michael, keep an eye open outside can you please?"

I opened the door and peered out looking both left and right.

"All clear," I said as I stuck my head back through the door. Martin quickly came out of the door with a black felt tip pen in his hand, and drew a small hash sign on the left-hand doorframe at roughly head height. We both then went back inside the room.

"Just a quick identification mark should we need it later," he said smiling.

"OK guys.

"That's it for now, there's nothing else to do until we come back here with the girls later today. Take your overalls off and roll them up. Hide both them, your hard hats and your goggles with the cases behind all the cable rolls."

We all did as we were told, left the room ensuring nothing was visible and casually made our way to the bank of lifts. The first lift to arrive had several workmen already inside it chattering away in either Arabic or Hindi. I don't know enough of either to be able to tell the difference, but we just ignored it anyway and carried on talking amongst ourselves with our backs to the lift so they hopefully wouldn't recognize us should they ever see us again. About 20 or 30 seconds later an empty lift arrived and the four of us got inside, changed lifts on the 40th floor, switching from the maintenance lifts to public lifts further along the same floor, and then rode to the ground floor and slowly walked out of the building mingling with the first visitors of thc day. Stage one had been successfully completed.

The four of us returned to the hotel and we passed the rest of the day quietly reading, watching TV, having a siesta or listening to music on headphones. About 4:00 p.m., we all left the hotel and all eight of us headed back to the Dubai mall in two taxis. Richard had issued a two-way radio set, complete with mics and earpieces to Martin, Helena and Sam. The cables disappeared into their pockets and they simply looked like they were listening to music on an mp3 player or their mobile phone. We arrived at the coffee shop opposite the entrance to the Burj Khalifa with plenty of time to spare, so we grabbed a coffee before joining the queue to go up to the viewing deck again. We slowly ambled forward every time a lift full of people departed, and we eventually got into the lift ourselves just before 5:30 p.m. We exited the lift in two different groups, each group totally ignoring the other. Martin, George, Colin and I were hovering at the souvenir counter near the doors Martin had looked behind yesterday, and Richard and the girls headed towards the security guard.

I couldn't hear what Sam and Helena were saying, but they'd obviously got his attention as he was soon busy pointing at something to the other side of the massive shop while Richard and Jo went and stood behind him blocking his view should he turn back towards us and the door we wanted to go through. Needless to say, with our guard looking the other way, we grabbed our opportunity and went through the door.

We were faced with a short passage, and then two flights of steps. One going up to our left, and one going down to our right. The steps of the stairs were a mixture of steel and wood, with strong handrails fitted on both sides, and like everything else in the building, very smart and very expensive looking. The stairs gave the impression of floating between floors with large air gaps between the stairs and the walls either side of them. On the inside were walls of sheet metal or beautiful wooden panels, and on the outside, walls of glass all the time reminding us just how high we were. We were starting on the 124th floor and we needed to get back to our storeroom on the 109th. It took about ten minutes, but it felt like thirty as we were dressed in civilian clothes and couldn't risk running or being spotted by security guards. The minute we reached the 109th floor we headed straight into our storeroom and bolted the door on the inside. We quickly got changed into our overalls and felt much better and somehow safer having now dressed in our 'disguises'.

The three girls and Richard had earlier in the afternoon managed to find out from the Burj Khalifa's reception desk what companies had corporate suites on the 111th and 112th floors.

They found the type of company they were looking for on the 111th and created a suitable sales pitch. The company they decided to target operating from the corporate suite was a small, but very exclusive travel company specializing in ultra-luxury tours to various parts of the world for the mega-rich. Sam and Helena had made an appointment and visited them at 6:30 p.m. that evening, taking Richard and Jo with them as two of their courier team, and they spent an hour pitching a selection of private concerts and exclusive parties using world famous groups, singers, orchestras etc. which they claimed they could provide exclusively to the company they were talking to. It was all rubbish of course, but they'd achieved what they wanted which was simply to get to the 111th floor legitimately without raising suspicion. At 7:30 p.m., they left the travel company, thanked them for their time, and closed the door behind them, but then instead of getting a lift down to the ground floor, they simply walked down a couple of flights to our storeroom, knocked on the door with the hash sign, and then using a previously agreed knock, they joined us behind the locked door. All we had to do now was wait until the early hours, and pray nobody wanted anything from our storeroom, and fortunately for us, they didn't.

We laid some clean painting sheets on the floor and took it in turns to grab a few hours of sleep, with two people staying awake while the others slept. Martin set his alarm for 1:30 a.m., and then shook me awake as I hadn't woken when it went off. We got the cases from the shelves and each member of the break-in team took the various bits of equipment we'd need. For that purpose, the white overalls were brilliant as Kurt had had half a dozen extra pockets added to the two pockets that came with the original design. George and Colin slid their aerosol cans into the thigh pockets on their right legs, with a slim, lightweight black rubber-covered metal cosh, and a powerful black rubber torch slotted into the other side pocket, just in case. Martin carried his various meters, magic boxes, tools, cameras, copiers etc. in three silver-colored metal cases, and these were distributed amongst the other three members of the break in team, and at five to two in the morning we opened the door of our storeroom, made sure it was clear outside, locked it behind us with a hasp and padlock George had fitted an hour earlier, and then all eight of us headed downstairs to the hundred and sixth floor, arriving at the luxury apartment of Ahmed and Nudara Bukhari.

There were surveillance cameras on every floor, one at the end of each corridor which were all dead ends, and the cameras were all mounted about eight feet up in the air. Martin kept us all well behind the camera while he walked up behind it, and then standing on a fold-up set of steps he'd brought with him, he took a photograph of the corridor from immediately above the camera, using a modern 'polaroid' style instant camera. It took about 15 seconds for the color print to emerge from the front of the camera, and he then clipped the picture into a magnetic bracket he'd also brought with him. Still standing on the top step, Martin lined up the picture in its bracket above the camera, and then quickly lowered it so that the magnets on the bracket clamped onto the surveillance camera holding the picture about six inches in front of the surveillance cameras. The view they would now have on the TV monitor in the security room would be identical to the real view Martin had just photographed, except we could now move around without being seen on the monitors as the photograph also showed the view down the corridor.

"OK. Positions everyone. Sam, I need you and Jo to stay here on lookout duty. From here, you'll be able to see the bank of lifts and both the up and down staircases. Use your radio and just let us know of any movement. If one of the lifts stops at this floor, or if you see anyone coming up or down the stairs, remove the picture in the bracket on top of the camera, then both of you hide in the cleaner's cupboard over there until whoever it is has gone. I unlocked the cupboard earlier and it now has a bolt fitted on the inside. Use it while you're in the cupboard. Colin will remove the bolt when we're finished. It will be tight but you should both just about fit in. Helena and Richard, once we're inside the apartment you two stay outside its door and warn me if anyone comes out of another apartment. As soon as you see or hear anyone you'll need to start getting amorous with each other. That should be enough to put anyone off talking to you or interrupting you. If Sam radios a warning about security guards approaching, dive inside the apartment. I'll leave it on the latch. Everyone clear? OK, I'll go first. As soon as I'm inside, George will go to Ahmed's room and Colin will go to Nudara's room and gas them both. Make sure you give them a good three second spray. Michael, bring up the rear, please."

Everyone took up their respective positions and Martin held one of his electronic gizmos against the door lock. He pressed a couple of buttons and after a few clicks, the red light on it changed to green. He held a finger to his lips and slowly opened the door. We knew at once that one of the brothers was in a deep sleep. You could hear his snoring at the door. A couple of table lamps with dimmers had been left on low in the living room, and these were enough that we didn't need to use our torches. In order to get to Ahmed's bedroom, George would have to walk straight ahead and then take the first left which led to both of the brother's bedrooms. Before anyone moved, Martin used another one of his metal gizmos and discovered a couple of pressure pads just inside the door. He disabled both and George then pulled the mask hanging round his neck up, so that it covered his nose and mouth, and crept forward into Ahmed's room and Colin turned right into Nudara's room. The snorer was Nudara. I stood by Nudara's bedroom door with a rubber truncheon in my right hand, just in case he woke up, but Colin, having pulled a mask over his own nose and mouth, quietly sprayed the Neothyl over the sleeping face. The snoring stopped and without doubt, he was unconscious. Colin left the room and I nodded to George who then opened the door into Ahmed's room. He quietly approached the bed with his truncheon in one hand and the aerosol in the other. Ahmed was obviously used to hearing his brothers snoring in the next-door bedroom, and in order to get to sleep, he had a pair of ear plugs neatly inserted. George sprayed Ahmed with a three-second burst of Neothyl and he too was now unconscious. With both brothers now well and truly out for the count, we exited both bedrooms; George and Colin removed their masks so that they could breathe easier and set about searching for information. Martin set up his portable copier on the coffee table, and opened one of the silver cases, this one with a green dot of paint near one of the locks. This simple color coding was Martin's way of identifying which case was which very quickly as all three cases were identical on the outside, except for a green dot, a blue dot and a red dot. The four of us then gathered around the coffee table.

"George, can you please try and find Ahmed's mobile, and bear in mind he may have more than one. Colin, likewise, please try and locate Nudara's. Make a very careful note of exactly where they are and how they're positioned, and then bring them back here."

George and Colin disappeared as Martin opened the case with the green dot. It was full to the brim with mobile phones of varying makes and models, each one with a short cable connected to it. Anticipating my question Martin said:

"Apple iPhones, Samsung Galaxys, Sonys, Motorolas, Nokias etc. Whatever mobile phone they've got I can plug it in to a matching phone here. I can then copy its contents straight onto an empty duplicate. It's very quick and it's simple, and they'll never know if the phones are put back exactly where they came from."

George returned fairly quickly with two phones. An iPhone and a cheap Nokia. Martin plugged them both in to his matching models and began transferring everything across.

"I suspect the Nokia is a cheap throwaway burner," said Martin. "But that's good if he has already loaded contact numbers into it."

"I can only find one phone," said Colin. "It's the latest Samsung Galaxy."

Martin dug out a Galaxy from the case and started transferring the information across.

"OK guys. Same thing, laptops and tablets. Note their position and bring them back here. Michael, can you please grab the red case, set up on the dining room table and get out three or four flash drives."

Inside the silver case with the red dot, Martin had three separate layers of grey sponge, each layer about an inch thick and each layer was glued to a black plastic tray beneath it. Sitting neatly in the top layer were 24 x Kingston Digital 1 Terabyte Data Traveler Ultimate GT USB Flash drives, all neatly slotted in 3 rows of 8. I didn't know it was possible to get that much information on one USB flash drive, but obviously it now was.

"I found an HP laptop," said George returning to the living room with it.

"And I've got an iPad," said Colin, holding it aloft and waving it in his hand.

“OK guys, take them over to Michael, grab a USB drive each and start copying absolutely everything you can find.”

Just then, Martin’s radio came to life with Sam’s voice whispering quietly.

“Security guards coming down the stairs. Jo and I have removed the bracket with the corridor photograph, and we are now in the cleaning cupboard. It’s bolted from the inside. Radio silence please everyone.”

At that moment, Richard and Helena came quietly through the front door which Helena locked behind her. She held her index finger to her mouth indicating total silence was now required from everyone. I stood stock still exactly where I was, feeling really nervous and I felt sure I was shaking like a leaf. Martin, George and Colin however had all sat down in the living room on the sofa or in the armchairs. They didn’t look in the least bit bothered by the security guards patrolling outside, and Martin had even started casually flipping through a magazine that had been laying on the coffee table. It seems funny how very late at night, or early in the morning as it was now, every little sound is greatly magnified. I could only just hear the guard’s footsteps on the ceramic tiled floor of the corridor, but I certainly clearly heard one of the guards try turning the handle of the cleaner’s cupboard and giving the door a sharp tug. I just prayed neither Sam nor Jo would make a noise and end up giving themselves away. It would seem that they didn’t, as just thirty seconds later, I could hear by their voices that the two guards were now outside the apartment, giving that door knob a twist and a pull. It had been locked by Helena as she and Richard came in, and the door didn’t budge. The two guards carried on chatting to each other as they slowly continued on their rounds, and the sound of their voices eventually faded and disappeared. Nobody moved or spoke for about a minute, although it felt much longer until we heard Sam’s voice over the radio again.

“All clear,” she whispered. “They’ve gone down a floor, and we’ve put the bracket back on top of the camera.”

Helena and Richard quietly let themselves out and went back on watch in the corridor, leaving the front door pulled to, but on the latch again.

Inside the apartment, Martin was the first to move and as he did so he issued commands.

"OK guys, back to work. George, copy the laptop please, Colin, likewise the iPad. Michael, see if you can find a PC anywhere, or any other computer devices."

From the dining room, I wandered into the maid's quarters, but we knew they didn't have a live-in maid, and from there I carried on into the kitchen where I found another laptop and a second iPhone, both sitting on the kitchen counter, both plugged in to the wall sockets and charging. I was about to grab them, but thought better of it. I returned to the living room.

"Martin, there's another laptop and another mobile, both on charge in the kitchen. What should I do with them?"

"Nothing," he replied. "What sort of phone is it?"

"Another iPhone." I replied, and grabbing a USB drive and a second duplicate iPhone from the first case Martin disappeared into the kitchen saying.

"Don't worry, I'll deal with them both. Have a look through the drawers of the desk against the wall over there and copy anything that looks interesting. Remember the rules?"

"I remember," I said smiling at him. When I'd first met Martin, we were in the Bahamas on another job for Interpol, trying to find the Mijas murderer. I nearly dropped us all in it more than once by forgetting the basic rules Martin had tried to drum into my thick skull. Don't move anything until you are 100% sure you can put it back exactly as you found it. Check all cupboard doors for contact pads before opening them, so on and so forth. There were seven basic rules and he'd made me learn them all. I knew the electronic scanner for checking the doors and windows was in the case with the blue dot and so I opened it, took it out, switched it on and went back to the desk. I held the scanner against the various drawers of the desk, and the drawers down both sides were all registering as clear. However, the wide center drawer showed a red light on the scanner indicating the presence of a contact pad. Martin had by now returned to the living room having left the laptop downloading onto a USB drive. I beckoned him over to the desk and pointed at the red light on the scanner. He smiled.

"Crafty buggers, these Arabs," he said.

"They obviously don't trust anyone."

Martin walked over to the same case I'd got the scanner from and pulled out a thin sliver of shiny metal about six inches long and two inches wide. He carefully inserted it between the top of the drawer and the underside of the desk top at the far-left side and slowly started sliding it from left to right. Just before half way along, the red light turned to green, but he kept sliding it along, and three inches later the green light turned red again. He continued to slide the sliver of metal, and just as it got to the far-right hand side, the red light went green again.

"I said they were crafty buggers, didn't I?" he said.

"Not content with one contact pad, there are two on this drawer. You have to be so damn careful."

"I know for a fact," I said, "that if had been me I would have assumed I'd found the contact pad, neutralized it and opened the drawer setting off the second contact pad and God knows what alarms."

"That's why I do this stuff and not you," Martin said, smiling at me.

"Can you get me a roll of masking tape out of the case please Michael, and another one of these?" he said, holding up the metal sliver.

Martin inserted the first sliver over the first contact pad and then did the same the other end with the second sliver. He then asked me to slowly slide the drawer open while he held them in place against the underside of the desk top. Apparently, the electronic sensors of contact pads are always attached to the desk itself, and never on the drawers. You learn something new every day! George and Colin had joined us by now and George, fully aware of what we were doing, tore off a couple of strips of masking tape and taped the left-hand sliver in position. He then did the same with the second one. That was enough to confuse the contact pads into thinking they were still touching. Inside the drawer were several books and papers. Martin opened the drawer all the way, and then using his instant camera again, he photographed the inside of the drawer. He now had a photograph of exactly where everything was in the drawer. He then got down on all fours, rolled over on to his back and shone his torch up onto the underside of the desk.

"Just checking for anymore contact pads," he said.

"OK, George, can you please start copying the contents of the drawer?" Martin said, getting back up from underneath the desk.

"Colin, can you please check that our two sleeping beauties are still in dreamland, and just to be on the safe side, give them another brief spray?"

"No problem," said Colin as he disappeared back to the bedrooms.

We spent another forty minutes in the apartment copying everything in sight. Exactly an hour after their first visit, the two security guards came back, still chatting and still tugging at doors. Sam and Jo had heard them coming again, warned us as before and then bolted themselves in the cleaner's cupboard again. Helena and Richard also reappeared, but this time everyone sat down a bit more relaxed having experienced this once already. Sam eventually gave us the all clear again about three minutes after they'd left.

"OK everyone," said Martin. "Let's wrap this up as soon as possible. I want to be out of here before the guards come back again. It looks like hourly patrols, so let's get moving."

We had by now copied anything and everything we could find, and that included a small black note book George found in Ahmed's bedside cabinet drawer. We had no idea what was in it as it was all handwritten in Ahmed's Arabic script, but George had photographed every page so that someone who did understand it could later give us the translation.

We very carefully put everything back exactly where we found it. George and Colin, using the photograph as a guide, put all the papers back in the desk drawer, and then I removed the masking tape while Martin held the slivers of metal in place, and once the drawer was finally back in place he removed the two slivers. The phones, laptops, tablets etc. had all been copied in their entirety and put back exactly where they came from, and at roughly 4:30 a.m., we all left the apartment exactly as we had found it. We picked up the other four team members and once Martin had removed his magnetic bracket with its corridor photograph from the top of the surveillance camera, we all headed back up the stairs to our storeroom where we quietly bolted ourselves in. Martin had slightly changed our original plan, and at 9:30 a.m. after all getting a couple of hours of sleep, the break-in team, still all dressed in our overalls, and now wearing our hard hats and safety goggles again, set off for the lifts. We were carrying between us our two rucksacks, plus the three silver metal cases, one of which contained all the papers we had photocopied now hidden in the false base of one of the cases. The four of us got into the lift, descended to the ground floor and slowly walked out through the staff entrance, casually chatting to each other, and waving at the guards, who then smiled at us and waved back.

"If only they knew," said George smiling.

Meanwhile, Richard and the three girls had got a lift to the 120th floor, walked the last few flights and emerged back in the shop on the observation floor around 10:00 a.m. They mingled with the crowd for a while, and then at 10:30 a.m. they descended back down to the ground floor and walked out with the rest of the morning's first visitors. We all met up in the coffee shop opposite the entrance and got two taxis back to our hotel. It had been a very long, but a very successful night.

Chapter Twenty

Once we'd got back to the Grand Hyatt, we all slept for a couple of hours, showered, got changed into fresh clothes and then reassembled in the lounge of my and Sam's suite.

"I think the logical thing while we're in the UAE," began Helena, "is to go and have a look at their offices in Abu Dhabi. I've no idea what we'll find, but it's got to be worth a try."

"Do we want to see what we've got from last night first?" I asked.

"No, I don't think so," said Helena. "If we do, we'll start trying to work things out, and we'll probably end up making decisions without knowing the full picture. Don't forget, a lot of what you guys collected last night is in Arabic, and we don't have a translator with us. Let's visit their offices in Abu Dhabi and see what we can find out from there."

"Do we have an exact address for their office?" Jo asked.

"Yes," replied Richard. "I've also got their GPS location, so it shouldn't be hard to find."

"Are we all going?" I asked. "Eight of us might seem like an invasion?"

"We'll all go to Abu Dhabi," said Helena, "and we'll fly the Gulfstream down there, but I think just you and Sam should go in first Michael, sound the place out, and see what the two of you can find out. A happy couple shouldn't be intimidating or suspicious."

"Cover story?" Sam asked.

"I suggest you make enquiries about the one and only business the brothers actually promote publically, which is highly exclusive and personal tours round the Sheikh Zayed Grand Mosque. Try and arrange a tour for all eight of us for the following day."

"What's so special about this mosque then?" asked Colin.

"The Sheikh Zayed Grand Mosque, that's its official title," began Helena, referring to a little black notebook she always carried with her, "is very special and quite unique, and as Paul's not here, it fell on me to do all the background research. A few basic facts for you: The carpet in the main prayer hall is the world's largest carpet. It measures 60,570 square feet, and was made in Iran by approximately 1,250 carpet knotters. The carpet weighs in total nearly 35 tons and it is mostly made of wool from New Zealand and Iran. According to the mosque's publicity, there are 2,268 million knots in the carpet and it took nearly two years to complete."

"Bloody hell," said Colin. "That's incredible.'

"Also, according to the mosque's publicity," continued Helena, "it can accommodate over 40,000 worshippers at the same time. The mosque also has three of the largest chandeliers in the world, each one containing millions of Swarovski crystals."

"This mosque is definitely open to the public, right?" I asked.

"Yes, but you have to show complete respect to all their traditions and clothing rules, particularly if you're not a Muslim. For example, all clothing for ladies must be loose fitting with long sleeves and ankle length skirts or trousers. No transparent clothing and no shorts for men. Women must wear a headscarf at all times and you can't wear your shoes inside the mosque. No PDAs or public displays of affection are allowed, i.e. no holding hands or kissing, definitely no smoking and no food is allowed inside the mosque either. According to my information, work started on the building in 1993 and it took eleven years to complete. I've seen loads of photographs and it really is a truly amazing place."

"OK," said George. "I get that this place is very special, and it's a really good front for the Bukhari brothers, but why are we all going to visit it?"

"Simple," replied Helena. "The Bukhari brothers' office is in the building next door."

We made our way to the airport, loaded everything on board the Gulfstream and then flew the short distance to Abu Dhabi International airport, this time with Colin at the controls.

We again checked in to a hotel, this time the Hyatt Capital Gate, which was one of those strange shaped buildings the UAE seemed to love. Sam and I left the others to unpack and settle in and we grabbed a taxi to the Bukhari brothers' office next to the mosque.

You can see the mosque from quite a distance, and I have to say without any shadow of a doubt, it is to my mind the most beautiful building I've ever seen. I don't get worked up particularly over architecture, but this place was, as Helena had said, rather special. Our taxi driver however drove straight past the mosque and pulled up outside the Bukharis' office. It wasn't as grand as the mosque next door, but it was nevertheless a very smart and quite opulent building. It was just two stories high, but like the mosque it was clad in pure white marble. We looked at each other, smiled and pushed the front door open.

"Good morning," I said as we approached the reception desk.

"Good morning sir, good morning madam," replied the receptionist, speaking perfect English. She was a very attractive Arab lady who was, I would guess, in her mid-thirties. She and a second, much younger girl with her, and both were dressed in western style business suits comprising of a bright red jacket and skirt over crisp white blouses, with their feet ensconced in white Jimmy Choo shoes. Well at least, Sam said they were. To me, shoes are shoes!

"I am Jamilah Almasi," she said. "This young lady is my assistant Leila, and how may we help you today?"

"Well," I began," our hotel, the Hyatt Capital Gate, told us that your company can organize personal accompanied tours of the Grand Mosque, and we wondered if you could arrange an accompanied tour for eight of us tomorrow?"

"Eight of you did you say, sir?' she asked. "Would there be any children in the group, as to be honest with you, our tours aren't really suitable for children."

"No, only my wife and myself, plus six business colleagues. We're only here for a couple of days and we would really like to see the mosque. As I said, this is quite a short trip and we only flew in to Abu Dhabi this morning," I said.

"Ah, the Etihad or British Airways flight, sir?' she asked.

"Oh neither," jumped in Sam. "We have our own Gulfstream, the latest G650ER."

The receptionist's attitude seemed to change immediately. She had been very polite to this point, but suddenly she became very friendly as well, but still with the same politeness.

"Well I'm sure we can organize a tour for tomorrow, sir. The full visit takes about three hours, but I assure you, you will not be bored."

"Will it be you that will be taking the tour or one of the Mr. Bukharis?" Sam asked. "I saw their two names above your door as being the owners. Father and son, I imagine?'

"No, Mr. Ahmed and Mr. Nudara are brothers, madam, and they own the business. Sadly however, they are not in the country at the moment and won't be returning until next week, so I'm afraid it will be me that takes you round tomorrow, if that's OK?"

"Oh, that's fine," I said jumping in. I could tell that Sam for some reason had taken an instant dislike to Miss Jamilah Almasi.

"Well in that case," she continued, "can I request that you all arrive here at ten in the morning please, and in the meantime please take this card with you, read it carefully and be sure to follow the Mosques rules about clothing and behavior. I am afraid they are very strict. Our fees are also printed on the card, and you can pay with any major credit card before we set off in the morning."

"Of course Jamilah," I replied. "Thank you so much for your help, and we look forward to the tour and seeing you tomorrow. Goodbye."

With her bidding us farewell, we left the building and caught a cab back to the hotel.

"I noticed that you weren't totally enamored with Miss Almasi," I began, sitting quietly in the back of the cab. "Any particular reason?'

"I know," said Sam. "And it's really strange, because I don't for the life of me know why. She was polite, she was friendly, and yet there was just something about her."

We changed the subject and chatted about other things on the way back to the hotel.

Chapter Twenty-One

We spent the rest of the day relaxing by the pool, and I don't think any of us had realized just how much stress we'd all been under at the Burj Khalifa. A swim, a few drinks and a very pleasant evening meal in the hotel's restaurant had brought us all back to life, and we were all now raring to go again. The following day after an early breakfast, we got two cabs and arrived at the Bukhari brothers' offices just before the appointed hour of ten o'clock.

Jamilah Almasi and her young female assistant were already there to greet us, but today Jamilah was dressed in traditional Arab costume, especially for the tour of the mosque. Her young assistant was still dressed in the smart red and white uniform of the previous day. Jamilah's outfit comprised of an abaya, which is a full-length kaftan or robe-like outer garment, which covered her entire body except for her head, hands and feet. Jamilah's abaya was the traditional black in color, but it also had beautiful gold embroidery decorating the shoulders, neck line and the ends of the sleeves. I have to say, it was a stunning garment and she looked incredibly elegant. She also wore a gold colored headscarf, known as a hijab, which was an essential requirement for all women who would be entering the mosque.

"Good morning ladies and gentlemen," she began. "I hope you enjoy our day together. If you don't mind I will quickly ensure everyone is suitably dressed before we head off, and please don't take offense. The UAE is a very relaxed and tolerant country compared to most Muslim countries, but the Sheikh Zayed Grand Mosque is our holiest building, and I am afraid we must all observe the mosque's rules."

"We completely understand," said Helena.

All eight of us had been very careful not to break any of the dress code rules printed on the card Jamilah had given us, as the last thing we wanted to do was cause any problems and draw attention to ourselves. Having got 'all clear' on the dress code, we walked from the office to the entrance to the mosque. Everybody was checked again by the security guards, and we saw two young ladies turned away from the entrance as they were both wearing standard western style dresses displaying an awful lot of their legs, and neither of them was wearing anything on their heads. Fortunately, they both had their arms covered in thin cardigans. The guard took them to a small 'waiting room' type area where he gave them both the loan of two full length skirts with elasticated waists and two headscarves.

"We do understand," said Jamilah, "that not everyone will be totally familiar with the mosque's rules on clothing, particularly Europeans and Americans, and so the mosque keeps a selection of garments to loan to visitors should they need them. I'm sure the two girls meant no offense, but I'm afraid they would not be allowed in the mosque showing their legs and with their heads not covered."

"Does that happen very often?" asked Sam. "People not wearing suitable clothes?'

"Oh, no more than a hundred times a day," laughed Jamilah. "As I said, it is mostly Europeans and Americans who have no knowledge of Muslim culture and Muslim laws."

We all entered the building and were staggered at the richness of the decoration. White marble and gold leaf everywhere. Truly stunning. For the next two hours, Jamilah gave us a lengthy and very knowledgeable description of everything we were seeing, and I have to say, she knew the answer to any question any of us threw at her. Sam had dropped back and was now walking and talking with Helena and Jo. Colin, George and Martin were bringing up the rear, and Richard and I were at the front with our guide.

"I hope you don't mind me asking this Jamilah, but surely your two bosses can't earn very much simply offering guided tours like this. Please don't get me wrong, this is really fascinating and well worth the money. I know it is not cheap, but even so, it would not be possible to do more than three tours a day. So, I assume they must have other businesses?"

"Yes of course. They are both very important businessmen and they have interests throughout the UAE, but they are also devout Muslims and they feel this part of their business empire

The Sheikh Zayed Grand Mosque in Abu Dhab

The Men's Prayer Hall in the Sheikh Zayed Grand Mosque

is very rewarding spiritually, if not quite so much financially. However, I'm sure you understand that I am not at liberty to discuss their private business."

"Oh, I'm sorry," I replied. "I meant no offense, it's just as I said, I find it difficult to imagine tours round the mosque would pay for your lovely offices and the staff."

Trying as hard as I could to get information out of her, she gave absolutely nothing away.

While we had been chatting, Colin had sped up and joined the girls, whereas Martin and George had slowly, and as previously arranged let us all get away from them. At the first opportunity they turned around, left the mosque and quickly and quietly walked back to Jamilah's office. My job now was to keep her occupied and hope she didn't realize two of our group had gone AWOL, and to that end we kept chatting for another ten to fifteen minutes. During a lull in the conversation, Richard suddenly said to our host.

"Can I ask you a personal question?"

"Of course," replied Jamilah. "You can always ask, but if it's too personal I hope you won't be offended if I refuse to answer you?" she laughed.

"Oh, well I just wondered if you were married?" asked an embarrassed Richard.

"No, I'm not," answered Jamilah. "Why, are you offering?" she teased.

Helena had overheard their conversation and piped up from the back.

"He's already spoken for Jamilah, so I'm afraid he's not offering."

"Oh well, never mind," sighed Jamilah, and everybody laughed.

"Have we lost George and Martin?" Jamilah suddenly asked noticing they were no longer with us.

"Oh, George said he needed some fresh air as he was getting a headache, and they said they'd meet us in the souvenir shop when we've finished the tour," replied Jo.

"Oh, OK," Jamilah said, but you could tell she wasn't very pleased.

We finished the tour about twenty minutes later in the souvenir shop where we found George and Martin sitting outside at a small round table drinking coffee. George apologized to Jamilah for leaving the tour early, and said he was now feeling so much better. As we'd already paid for the tour before we'd left, we simply said our goodbyes to Jamilah, and she returned to the office. We climbed into two taxis and made our way back to the hotel where we all then gathered for a quick debrief from Martin and George.

"When we reached the office," began Martin. "There was still only Leila, the young girl there. So George here played the poor, distressed, fainting warrior, dropped to the floor and when he came around asked for some water. While Leila went off to get some, I plugged a super-fast USB flash drive into her computer and downloaded everything on it. I'd just about managed to retrieve it before she returned. It may well have nothing of any great importance on it, but at least we've got it, and more importantly, they don't know we've got it."

"Also," said George, "I managed to photograph a book on her desk with loads of telephone numbers in it. Again, may be useful and maybe not."

"Well done guys," said Helena. "I don't think there's anything more we can do here in Abu Dhabi, so let's get back to the plane and head for stage three, the brothers' warehouses outside Muscat, in Oman."

Chapter Twenty-Two

Oman is an ancient Arab country on the southeastern coast of the Arabian Peninsula. It holds a strategically important position at the mouth of the Persian Gulf, and shares land borders with the United Arab Emirates to the northwest, Saudi Arabia to the west, and Yemen to the southwest. Oman also has marine borders with both Iran and Pakistan.

The capital of Oman is Muscat, and we landed at Seeb, Muscat's international airport, and George taxied us into a large hangar reserved for keeping private aircraft out of the scorching sun. A customs officer gave the plane a quick inspection, but finding nothing untoward he gave us a clearance document and left us in peace.

"OK," began Helena as we all seated ourselves in the main cabin of the aircraft. "Our job here is very simple. The brothers have a series of warehouses right on the coast about fifteen minutes' drive north of Muscat. We need to get into those warehouses and try to find out what they do there. Martin, over to you."

"Thanks Helena. I suggest we stick to the same teams and same routines we used at the Burj Khalifa, i.e. I will go in with Michael, George and Colin, while the rest of you keep watch and let me know what's happening by radio."

"Do we know if there are any guards?" asked Colin.

"No, we have no idea at this stage, which is why we're going to go on a stake out tonight. We need to find a flat roof where we can watch the warehouses all night through binoculars, and then make timing notes of any guards, patrols, night-watchmen etc. The four of us will be sufficient for that. Two-hour shifts of two people. Starting at eleven thirty, Martin and I will go first and then we'll swap with George and Colin every two hours. We need to find the quietest time, but be well away by six in the morning."

"If all goes well," said Helena, "we go in tomorrow night."

"By a stroke of luck," said Richard, "it appears that the two Bukhari brothers are also here in Oman and staying at the Chedi hotel here in Muscat. I wondered if it might be worth following them today and see whom they meet and what they're up to."

"How the hell do you know they're here?" asked Jo.

"I put untraceable tracking software onto both of their main mobiles while we were copying all their data," said Martin.

"Richard brought the software with him on a memory stick and gave it to me before we broke in at the Burj. To be strictly honest, we only know where their mobiles are, but that should mean we know where they are as well."

"Well done Richard," said Helena. "Good thinking."

"Oh, I'm not just a pretty face, you know," he said.

"Is your mirror broken?" I jokingly asked him.

"Kindly don't be mean to my husband," said Helena, jumping in and rebuking me.

"I think you've got a pretty face, and a pretty mind," she said. "Ignore the nasty man dear."

"So where is this Chedi hotel?" asked Sam laughing at the banter.

"It's on the Boushar beachfront, right here in Muscat," replied Richard. "It's just a short distance from here."

"OK Sam," said Helena. "Why don't you, Jo and I go to the Chedi hotel and see if we can follow them. We can play tourists and leave all the guys here to sort out their various boys-toys for tonight's stake out and tomorrow's break in."

"Sounds like a plan," replied Sam, and the girls got ready and called a taxi.

The five of us men that had been left behind spent the next two hours preparing everything for the next two nights, when a taxi pulled up outside the hangar. The three girls got out and they were all looking extremely fed up.

"Problem?" queried George as they approached the Gulfstream.

"Bloody Arabs," cursed Jo as the three of them climbed the steps and came on board. "Why the hell can't they wear sensible different-colored clothes like everybody else, instead of all wandering about the streets in white night shirts and tea towels?"

"In other words, you lost them," said Colin, and we all started laughing.

"Oh, we found them OK," began Sam. "They were both staying at the Chedi, which is a gorgeous hotel by the way, and we saw them at the hotel's bar. So, we sat down about twenty feet away from them, and had an ice-cold coke while keeping an eye on them."

"After about fifteen minutes," said Helena, "they got up and wandered out of the hotel and into the local market. We followed them immediately, to try and see if they met with anyone, but after five minutes we started arguing amongst ourselves as to who was who, and was it them, or was it somebody else."

"They were both wearing white dishdashas and cream massars," said Sam.

"The trouble is," said Jo, "so was everybody else. It was impossible to follow anyone, particularly from behind them as they all looked the same."

"Sorry to ask," said Richard, "but what are dishdashas and massars?"

I knew the answer to this and felt confident enough to respond to the question.

"A dishdasha," I began, "is a simple, ankle-length, collarless gown with long sleeves, and they are usually white in color. Nearly all men wear them when outside the house."

"And a massar?" asked Richard.

"You have to understand," I replied, "Oman is one of the hottest countries in the world and no sensible man ever ventures outside without wearing a headdress of some sort, or the top of his head will get totally fried. The Omanis wear either a round cap called a kumma, or a cashmere kerchief called a massar, or quite often a combination of both where the massar is wound over and round the kumma."

"Both of the brothers," said Helena, "were wearing pure white dishdashas and cream colored massars over their kummas, as were most of the other men in the market. It was simply impossible to tell who was who, so we eventually gave up and got a taxi back here."

"So, were all the women in black burqas?' asked Colin.

"Oh no," replied Sam. "We only saw a couple of burqas. The women mostly wear a kandoorah, which I was reliably told by one of the shopkeepers is a long tunic style dress. They are made in a variety of stunning colors on which the bodice area and the long sleeves have incredibly beautiful hand-stitched embroidery of various designs and colors, but most frequently in gold or silver stitching. Similar to what Jamila was wearing at the Mosque. Sometimes instead they wear loose fitting trousers, tight at the ankles called sirwals, and these are worn underneath a dishdasha. On their heads they wear a lihaf, which is a posh name for what is basically a fancy shawl."

"In case you're wondering how we know all this," said Jo, "we went into a very smart garment shop where they made all these clothes after we lost the brothers in the market, and stood and watched one of the craftsmen at work, while the lady in the shop explained it all to us. They are so clever and skilled."

"Well, never mind," said Martin, "we don't actually need to follow them or even know where they are in order to do tonight's job of surveillance. Can I suggest we get a bit of shut eye and head for the warehouse about eleven o'clock tonight?"

"I hope you don't mind Michael," said Sam once we'd moved to the back of the plane and settled down in a couple of armchairs.

"But I bought a beautiful royal blue kandoorah with fabulous gold stitching. I've no idea when or where I'll wear it, but I just couldn't resist. It's simply the most beautiful dress I've ever seen."

"Of course, I don't mind," I replied. *Well, I ask you. What was I supposed to say?*

We found the warehouses with no trouble, there were in fact three of them, and dressed in our all-black outfits we all merged into the darkness. We found a flat roof on a two story building about quarter of a mile away, and settled down for the night. We'd brought two sets of binoculars on short tripods with us, and Jo had provided us with thermoses of hot sweet tea, a dozen pork pies and a dozen jam donuts from the Gulfstream's fridge. Apparently, George loves his pork pies and Colin loves his jam donuts, and Jo had stocked up on both before leaving.

There were two security guards patrolling the area around the warehouses, but they didn't seem to have a set routine or route, and they frequently stopped for a smoke and a chat.

By four in the morning Martin decided he'd seen enough, so he and I went down from the roof and the two of us dodged between buildings on our way to the brothers' warehouses. Martin needed to find a door or a window through which we could enter the following night. After ten minutes of dodging and diving in response to George's radio warnings, we finally made it to the back of the nearest and biggest of the warehouses.

"Sorry Martin, but can you please get down on your hands and knees. I need to stand on your back and look through the window."

I did as requested and Martin got his look through the glass. He was back down on the ground again in thirty seconds.

"There's a night watchman in there," said Martin, "but he appears to be fast asleep. Getting in through the window will be a doddle, and I can't see any alarms."

"Sounds great," I muttered, not sure if I was happy about this or not.

"OK everyone, let's go," Martin said into his radio, and he and I slowly and carefully made our way back to the bottom of the stairs that had led up to our watching roof. George, Colin and Richard had all come down to join us on Martin's instructions, and we made our way back to the car and then drove gently and calmly back to the hangar. We were all sleeping on the plane as it could easily accommodate all eight of us in the various armchairs, of which every two worked together in pairs much like sofa beds did, and they made very comfortable beds. The girls were all asleep when we returned, but Helena woke as we opened the plane's door and came aboard. She saw it was us, waved, muttered something unintelligible, and then just rolled over and went back to sleep.

The following day we did very little, but in the evening, we prepared and checked all the equipment again, and then at eleven o'clock sharp we headed back to the warehouses. As before at the Burj, Martin, Helena and Sam all had radio headsets on, and all eight of us were dressed in black from head to toe. Martin led the way, with me behind him, Sam and Jo followed, with Helena and Richard behind them, and finally George and Colin bringing up the rear. Martin had brought the Gulfstream's small pair of black metal steps with him this time, and once the guards had gone he set them up under the window, climbed them, and within thirty seconds he had the window ajar. He quietly slid inside as I climbed up behind him and watched. He slowly crept up to the night watchman, who was definitely not watching, but quietly dozing. Martin gave him a few seconds spray of Neothyl, and then beckoned the rest of us to join him. In quick succession, myself, George and Colin climbed through the window, Colin closed it behind him and Richard picked up the steps and went and joined the girls who were watching out for the patrolling guards.

Martin had asked the girls to let him know when the guards were more than a hundred yards from our warehouse, at which point we could turn on our torches and start nosing around. We got the signal from Sam and four torches immediately came to life and gave off four slim pure white beams. The warehouse was stacked with hundreds of long wooden crates, each one about six feet long, although some were even longer. In one corner was a large wooden desk against the wall, with a cork noticeboard attached to the wall above it.

Martin told us to investigate what was inside the crates while he checked out the desk. George and Colin joined me, and both Colin and I picked up crowbars from the floor and started prising open the lids of various crates while George held the torches so we could both see what we were doing. What we found inside those crates horrified us all. Various types of SAMS or surface to air missiles, a massive selection of automatic machine guns, various hand guns, various types of grenades, shoulder born bazookas and worst of all, thousands of canisters of both mustard gas and sarin gas. Martin had come over and joined us, and he very quickly took in everything we'd seen from the crates we'd opened, and he immediately instructed us to as quietly as possible fasten all the lids back down, and then we left the warehouse same way we'd come in, being careful to leave everything just as we'd found it. Thirty minutes later we were all back on the aircraft, and ten minutes after that, Colin lifted off and we headed back to the sanity of the UK.

Chapter Twenty-Three

Back in Greenwich, Richard took two full days to go through and collate everything we'd found on the various phones, laptops, tablets, papers, books etc. in Dubai, Abu Dhabi and Oman. The rest of us used that time to rest and get our energy back. On Wednesday morning, we all assembled back in Stephen's office minus Martin, who having completed his work had flown to Cyprus to do another covert job for Kurt. Paulo had flown in from the Algarve and Kurt joined us from Amsterdam via the TV monitor.

"Thank you, everyone," began Stephen. "I gather from Richard that there is an amazing amount of information to go through, a lot of which is incredibly worrying, and therefore this meeting could last all day."

"I have organized a running supply of tea and coffee," said Paul. "Although I can't really help you with that Kurt."

"Don't worry Paul," replied Kurt. "I have my own team of Dutch slaves to pander to my every need here in Amsterdam."

"Can we get on gentlemen, please?" asked an impatient Stephen. "Richard, you have done all the collation work on this, so over to you."

"Thank you, sir," began Richard.

"It has taken me a couple of days to put all this together, and I have to admit some of this is conjecture on my part, but it is all based on the facts we found in the various locations. Can I start by stating what to most of us has become blindingly obvious? Ahmed and Nudara Bukhari are without doubt illegal arms traders, supplying weapons of every kind to terrorist organizations around the world. Amongst the information we found on Ahmed's laptop was their client list, both past and current. To make life easier for us all, I've typed them up in an alphabetical order and printed a copy for everyone, but while we're talking I'll also put the list up onto the screen."

Richard passed an A4 sheet with his list on to everyone in the room, and then the self-same list appeared on the large TV monitor. It read as follows:

Al-Qaeda, Al-Shabaab, Boko Haram, Hamas, Harkat-ul-Mujahideen, Hezbollah, ISIS, The Muslim Brotherhood, Palestinian Islamic Jihad and the Taliban.

"Good God," said Stephen. "I knew it was bad, but this is horrendous."

"Can you email me all this please Richard?" asked Kurt.

"Of course, sir," he replied.

"For goodness' sake Richard," said Stephen. "Stop calling us all 'sir' during these meetings. I said ages ago that we are all equal team members, unless of course we're down to the last biscuit, at which point I will obviously pull rank."

"Do we know, Richard?" began Sam. "Whether they have actually supplied all these groups, or is this just a list of potential clients?"

"Oh, they have supplied them all right. Amongst one of the ledgers on the laptop was a list of exactly what weaponry has been supplied to which group, when it was purchased and how much was paid. It seems that the brothers are far wealthier than we originally thought, and in fact they have to date banked in excess of 12 billion US dollars in various numbered bank accounts all over the world. They have accounts in the Caymans, the Bahamas, Belize, Switzerland, Lebanon, Lichtenstein, Monaco and Singapore. I should point out by the way, that this information was also gleaned illegally by us from Ahmed's laptop in their apartment at the Burj Khalifa in Dubai."

"I'm not concerned about infringing the civil rights of these bastards," said Stephen.

"Do we have any account numbers or passwords?" asked Paul.

"Afraid not," replied Richard. "Although there are what we think are a load of codes in Arabic, all written in a black notebook that was in Ahmed's bedside cabinet, but at this stage I haven't been able to break any of it as I don't speak the lingo. I will send a copy to you Kurt if that's OK. I know some of your chaps are brilliant at this sort of thing."

"Of course," replied Kurt.

"Do we know how they get their hands on all this weaponry?" I asked.

"Yes, we do," replied Richard. "And that leads me onto one excellent item of news. We now have a name for the Faro Forger. He currently works exclusively for the two brothers and produces whatever they want. The counterfeit currency was produced in order to get the project off the ground. That money was laundered into real, genuine cash, and that cash was used to purchase all the weaponry which was then sold on to the terrorist organizations with, from what I can tell, at an average mark-up of eight hundred percent."

"Don't keep us in suspense Richard," said Helena.

"Who is the Faro Forger?"

"He's actually one of your countrymen Helena. A Mr. Cornelius Janssen, who comes from a small town called Barendrecht not far from Rotterdam, although he left there years ago and he now operates from either Dubai where he creates all the plates, or Faro where everything is printed. We think he is currently in Dubai, but we don't know exactly where."

"So, back to my question," I repeated. "Where do they get all this weaponry?"

"Sorry Michael," said Richard. "Most of it is obtained by using forged documentation, and that's where the Faro Forger comes in. Cornelius Janssen produces a document that is required by all companies selling arms anywhere in the world, and that's called an end user certificate. Let's say for example the government of Botswana issues an end user certificate stating that they wish to purchase 500 machine guns and 500,000 rounds of ammunition for their army. They present the supplying company with an end user certificate and if the supply company is happy with the certificate's authenticity they will then happily supply the weapons. That's why the Faro Forger is so important. Some countries' arms industries insist on far more paperwork and far more rigorous checks than others, and so usually weapons traders deal with countries whose paperwork requirements are minimal."

"So, who are the main supply countries?" asked Jo.

"There is a whole host of arms suppliers. The biggest two in the world are the USA, and Russia. China is now up to third place, with the highest ranking European country being France which comes in at number four. Germany, the UK and Spain all do a fair bit of business at five, six and seven, with Italy at eight, the Ukraine and Israel completing the world's top ten suppliers. Of these, Russia, China and the Ukraine are the easiest to get weapons from as countries like the USA and the UK have very strict controls."

"I saw on the list of weapons you found in Oman, hundreds of canisters of both mustard and sarin gas. Surely they are banned all over the world?' queried Stephen.

"Yes, they are," replied Richard. "There are numerous treaties such as the Geneva Protocol which dates right back to 1925, the Biological Weapons Convention which came into force back in 1975, and the Chemical Weapons Convention of 1993. Then there's the fairly recent Arms Trade Treaty which came into force on Christmas Eve 2014."

"I suppose the problem is," said Paul, "that the people and countries who abide by all these treaties are basically the good guys, but treaties have never made any difference to terrorist organizations or despots like Pol Pot, Idi Amin, Saddam Hussein etc."

"The innocent people of Syria now know all about mustard gas as well," said George.

"Exactly."

"Kurt, can I arrest this Cornelius Janssen next time he sets foot in Faro?' asked Paulo. "Or do you want me to leave him free to operate at the moment."

"To be honest Paulo I'm not sure at the moment. For everyone's sake, we need to shut their operation down as fast as possible, but I need to see how much evidence can be used in court. As Richard said earlier, most of what we have was obtained by illegal but sadly very necessary methods, and as such, we can never use any of it in a court room. Let me think on that one and come back to you."

"Doesn't Interpol have a hit squad that could take the brothers out and save us all a lot of time and money?" I asked. "You know, the loss of two lives in order to save thousands."

"I understand your sentiments Michael," said Kurt. "And I agree that people who sell mustard gas, sarin gas and surface to air missiles to terrorists have no right to the niceties of life, but that sort of thing is way beyond my jurisdiction."

"I'm surprised at you Michael," said Stephen. "Assassinations? Is that really you speaking, or is it just your feelings of enacting justice in its simplest form?"

"Sorry everyone," I said. "It just gets to me that these two guys have now become multi-billionaires by providing the means for thousands of innocent men, women and children to be slaughtered in the name of one terrorist group or another. I hate this feeling and I can't at the moment see how they're going to be brought to justice!"

"I see where you're coming from," replied Stephen. "But we have to be the good guys."

"I remember seeing a film years ago," I said, "where Oliver Reed ran this organization called 'The Assassination Bureau'. It was a brilliant, but at the same time a very silly film, and every now and again I wonder if it wouldn't be good to just hand a list of names to such an organization and let them do their stuff."

"And who would decide what names go on the list?" asked Sam frowning at me.

I knew I was on a loser, but I still wanted to make my point.

"Oh, I do," I proclaimed. "It's my idea and it would be my list. There'd be Kim Jong-un on it for a start. Surely, everyone agrees that the world would be a much safer place without him in it. Then there's the ISIS leader Abu Bakr al-Baghdadi. He would certainly be no loss to the world. I know it's crazy and I'm not seriously advocating assassination, but you can't help wondering sometimes if it wouldn't be the easiest way of solving some of the world's major problems. Sorry folks, rant over and back to serious matters."

"Well, thank you for that most interesting diversion Michael," said Stephen in his most sarcastic voice.

"Can you tell us please Richard what physical evidence we have that can actually be used in court?"

"Of course," he replied.

"The simple answer is none. Everything we know and everything we have was obtained through illegal breaking and entering and trespassing. We sprayed knock out gas on people while they were asleep, we illegally copied their private information etc. I'm sorry, but we have nothing that can be used in a trial. Any judge would throw it all out."

"In that case," said Kurt, "we have to catch them in the act and close them down that way. I think we're going to have to run some kind of sting on them."

Chapter Twenty-Four

"Will the UAE authorities cooperate with us?" asked George.

"Oh, most certainly," said Paul. "The UAE strongly condemn terrorism and extremism in all its forms. I've been to the UAE several times over the last few years and know a few police officers in both Dubai and Abu Dhabi. They work very closely with the United States and several other countries, and they have no problem demonstrating their commitment to confront, degrade and eradicate terrorism and extremism right across the Middle East, and worldwide for that matter."

"But does that mean they'll cooperate with us?" repeated George.

"Definitely, providing we don't break any of their laws without their permission," replied Paul. "As we speak The UAE is actively participating with the USA and other coalition partners in the fight against ISIL/Daesh. They've also contributed a lot to the fight against terrorism and extremist movements such as Al Qaeda, Hezbollah, the Taliban, the Houthis, and Al-Shebaab. Although small in number, they still continue to deploy their forces in Afghanistan, Somalia and Yemen in the fight against terrorists and extremists. I think we can safely say they will support us providing we work with them and don't go behind their backs."

"If I can interrupt you Paul," said Kurt. "Having now thought this through, can I suggest that what we have here is in fact two very separate aims and objectives? One is apprehending and stopping the work of our Faro Forger, Mr. Cornelius Janssen and his gang of printers. That is something we can deal with relatively easily, and it is something we have authority to deal with. However, the second aim is to stop the Bukhari brothers and their associates from supplying arms to terrorists, and we do not have jurisdiction in this matter as it involves the UAE and Oman, both of which are outside Europe, and we do not have the necessary manpower – they do. I suggest that if they are agreeable, we meet with the UAE police as soon as possible and share everything we know with them. If they invite us to stay involved then fine, but I strongly feel that we have to hand the arms aspect of this investigation over to them. The people we are dealing with here are very serious about what they do, and I'm sure they won't think twice about killing anyone who gets in their way. So far, we've been very lucky. Let's keep it that way and not push our luck."

"I wholeheartedly agree," said Stephen. "We've been incredibly fortunate that nobody has been caught breaking and entering, and…"

"Er, excuse me Stephen," I interrupted, "there was no breaking. Just a bit of entering."

"Oh, I do most humbly apologize Michael, please forgive my gross misinterpretation of your actions on behalf of law and order."

"Steady on Stephen," said Sam leaping to my defense. "Michael was only joking."

"I know, and so am I. Good grief you two, relax will you? I think you're all doing a great job. Now, can I suggest Paul and Kurt arrange a meeting with the police inspector Paul knows in Dubai, and then you Paul, along with Helena, George, Colin, Michael and Sam go back to Dubai, meet Kurt there who can add Interpol authority, and you can then brief the police in Dubai, Abu Dhabi and Oman on everything you've all discovered over the last few weeks? Meanwhile, I will stay here and work with Richard, Jo and Paulo and put together a strategy for the arrest and conviction of our Faro Forger and his team of merry men in time for your return."

"Sounds like a plan," said Helena, and we adjourned the meeting much earlier than we originally thought.

The following day, Kurt flew in from Amsterdam and joined us in Paul's office. Sam and I were there along with Helena, George and Colin, and we all sat round a large conference table while Paul was talking to his police contact in Dubai. Eventually, he replaced the telephone.

"As you've just heard, I've had a lengthy conversation with Inspector Khalid Alfarsi, my friend in the Dubai police. As a result of that conversation, he has arranged a meeting for tomorrow afternoon with his big boss in Dubai, Police Brigadier Murad El Hashem, and his counterpart in Abu Dhabi, Police Brigadier Sharif Saqqaf. I've told Khalid roughly what we've discovered, but not at this stage how we got the information. I thought that could probably wait until we're face to face with them."

"I assume I'm flying us out there on the company bus?" said George.

"Correct," said Paul. "I think it's my turn to be pampered and experience the lifestyle of the rich and famous that Michael and Sam are now becoming accustomed to."

"Sorry, Paul," said Kurt. "Jo is staying here in Greenwich, so you'll have to pour your own gin and tonics."

"Preposterous," spluttered Paul. "What is the world coming to?" and we all laughed.

We landed in Dubai around midday and were met in the main terminal by Police Inspector Khalid Alfarsi, a handsome man in his mid-thirties who immediately reminded me of Omar Sharif during the filming of Lawrence of Arabia. Sam and Helena both commented on how good looking he was. Khalid was dressed in smart western clothes of beige-colored slacks and an open necked white shirt which helped show off his remarkable tan. Khalid had first trained as a police officer at Hendon in England, which was where he and Paul had first met, then once he'd completed his training he headed back to Dubai. He shook hands with us all as Paul did the introductions, and he then guided us straight out of the airport and into a waiting silver-colored Mercedes mini bus. Khalid sat in the front seat next to his driver, and the rest of us all piled into the back. He turned in his seat to face us all.

"Welcome to Dubai, all of you. Although from what Paul has just told me while we were walking from the airport to the car, you were all here, how shall we say, 'incognito' quite recently?"

"Not me," said Paul. "It was them what did it your honor," he laughed.

"Please don't worry about it," soothed Khalid. "We have no patience with people like the Bukhari brothers, and it seems to me that everything you did was completely necessary. I see your colleague Martin is not here with you, Kurt. A great pity."

“Why?” asked Sam. “Did you want to arrest him?”

“Good grief, no,” Khalid exclaimed. “I wanted to offer him a job.”

“You leave Martin alone,” laughed Kurt. “He’s a bit special and I’d have a hell of a job trying to replace him. Besides, why on earth would Martin be interested in coming to a miserable place like this, with nothing to offer except glorious sun, endless white sandy beaches, beautiful women, a wonderful lifestyle, and pots of money to throw around?”

“Yes, I see your point,” smiled Khalid. “I would be wasting my time.”

“Being serious for a moment,” I said. “Can you tell us please Khalid a little about the two Police Brigadiers we are meeting this afternoon. Will they be as relaxed about how we obtained all this information as you are?”

“Well, my own boss, Brigadier Murad El Hashem, is great, and he will be fine. As for Brigadier Sharif Saqqaf, he is a bit more of a stickler for the rules, and I don’t think he will take too kindly to the breaking and entering aspect of your visit.”

I was about to mention my joke about the non-breaking, only entering, again, but Sam kicked me on the shin and whispered.

“Don’t you ever know when to keep quiet, Michael?”

I felt suitably chastised, but spoke anyway.

“Actually Khalid, we did nothing illegal in Abu Dhabi other than copy a few bits of information from a computer onto a memory stick, and I assume what we did at the Burj Khalifa in Dubai is a matter for the Dubai authorities and nothing to do with Abu Dhabi?”

“Correct, Michael. And Moory, sorry, that’s what we call Brigadier Murad El Hashem, he won’t have a problem with it at all. I suggest you just don’t mention the memory stick at all and simply say you just had a conversation with Miss Almasi, and she accidentally let some things slip in conversation.”

“What do we do about Oman?” asked Kurt. “That’s where all the arms are located.”

“Actually,” said Khalid, “we have an excellent working relationship with the Omani authorities. Khasab is a small coastal town in an area of northern Oman named Musandam which is separated from the rest of Oman by UAE territory, and at its closest point it is only 30 miles across the straits of Hormuz to Iran. Needless to say, a lot of smuggling goes on between the two, mostly using very fast speedboats. Over the years the UAE has worked closely with the Omanis, and to be honest the smugglers are mostly left alone now to get on with it, providing they stick to smuggling TVs and DVD players. However, both the UAE and Oman draw the line on drug smuggling, and we clamp down on that and work very closely together on arrests. So far, we have been reasonably successful."

"So how do we approach the Omanis," asked Kurt?'

"You don't," replied Khalid. "We'll do that and propose a joint operation between the UAE and Oman. I'm afraid the Sultan of Oman, decent chap though he is, would not take kindly to Interpol or any other outside authorities getting involved in what he will see as a purely internal affair."

"That's fine by us," said Kurt. "As long as something is done to stop the Bukharis, we don't really care who does it. However, we would like to see it through and see them brought down if possible."

"Oh, I'm sure Brigadier Murad El Hashem will happily let you, Kurt, and your team come along as observers, but you must promise not to get involved and start any international incidents."

"No problem," replied Kurt on behalf of all of us, while looking at me!

We arrived at the general headquarters of the Dubai Police, in Al Nahda Road in the Al Twar district of Dubai. A spectacular building of concrete, steel, white tile and glass that reminded me in style of the cream and green MI6 building located on the Thames in London, although this was much bigger and far grander. While we were waiting for the two Brigadiers, Khalid gave us some background information on the Dubai Police.

"I have to say," he began, "that we are, in my opinion, without doubt the most forward thinking and progressive Arab police force today. We employ over seventeen thousand officers, all of the highest educational standards of any organization in the Arab world. We were the first Arab police force to apply DNA testing in criminal investigations, the first to use electronic finger printing, and the first Arab department to apply electronic services. We also use GPS systems to locate Police Patrols via satellite which greatly helps in aiding operations."

Dubai Police Headquarters

Aerial View of Dubai Police Headquarters

Before any of us had a chance to comment, a young police officer asked us all to follow him into the command and control room, where one of the two Brigadiers was waiting for us.

I was really not prepared for what greeted us. The police's command and control room in their Dubai headquarters was not so much a room as a small auditorium, and to my mind it was a cross between NASA's Mission Control Centre at Houston and the HQ of any of the power crazed mad villains in a James Bond film. The entire wall across the front of the room was taken up with massive screens showing CCTV footage from all over Dubai, and positioned in front of the screen were, I estimated, 50 or 60 computer operators, all seated in tiered rows much like in a theatre, and each one of them had two computer screens and a keyboard in front of them as well as a telephone. Brigadier Murad El Hashem was like Khalid, a handsome man with brown hair and a well-trimmed moustache, and I estimated he was in his mid-forties. He greeted us warmly, shook all our hands, and proudly showed us round the command and control room before leading us into a large conference room off the side, where his colleague from Abu Dhabi was already seated and waiting for us.

The standard uniform of the Dubai police is an olive-green shirt with a red band running under the left arm and looped through the left epaulette, a dark green beret with a gold badge depicting the logo of the police force, olive green trousers and black boots. Women officers generally wear a headscarf due to Islam being the official religion of the state. However, high-ranking officers such as Brigadier Murad El Hashem wear a light brown uniform with the olive-green trousers and black boots, and a very smart cap on their heads instead of the beret, and rank badges on their collar. All police officers in Dubai carry semi-automatic handguns, either a Caracal or the more usual Sig Sauer pistol, and Moory was no different. Brigadier Sharif Saqqaf turned out to be everything Murad El Hashem wasn't. Moory was tall and elegant, Saqqaf was short and if I'm honest, a bit tubby, Moory had a very smart moustache, Saqqaf just had a lot of stubble on his chin. Moory's uniform was very smart and well pressed, Saqqaf's uniform was scruffy with sweat marks under his armpits. I have to be honest and say I didn't really take to Brigadier Sharif Saqqaf.

We all sat round the conference table and after all the introductions had been completed, Kurt took the lead, explaining why we had started investigating the brothers, and with input from Helena, Paul, George and me, we told them everything we had discovered. Moory asked a couple of very relevant and quite sensible questions, whereas Saqqaf was very much old school Arab, and he just sat there looking daggers at both Helena and Sam. He did not like women having any role in life other than serving men and producing children. His view was that women should have no authority and he definitely couldn't stand the fact that Helena's rank was equivalent to his. The meeting drew to a close with Saqqaf informing us he didn't think there was any point in Abu Dhabi being involved in this affair as it was nothing to do with his jurisdiction, and he felt we'd just wasted his very valuable time. His view was that the two brothers both lived in Dubai and they traded their arms from Oman where they are all housed, and with that he got up, shook hands with Kurt, glowered at Helena and Sam, and then bid us all farewell and left.

"Well that was fun, wasn't it?" said Moory breaking the ice, and we all laughed. "Brigadier Sharif Saqqaf is, I'm afraid very fond of the old ways and he really does not approve of how life has changed in the twentieth century, never mind the twenty first, but in a way, he is right. We and the Omanis can deal with this matter between the two of us."

"Thankfully," said Khalid. "Brigadier Saqqaf retires at the end of the year, and his replacement is very different. Now regarding the Bukharis – may I suggest sir that we start by hitting the brothers where it will hurt them most. We could completely disrupt their illicit financing by the immediate freezing of all their bank accounts here in Dubai, and ask all other countries where we now know they have accounts to do the same, plus I suggest we also take away their passports immediately while our investigations proceed."

"Can you really do that?" asked Paul.

"Who the hell's going to tell us we can't?" said Khalid with a laugh.

"An excellent idea," said Moory. "Will you see to it immediately please, Captain? In the meantime, gentlemen, and ladies of course, can I offer you a little late lunch in our staff restaurant which is of course excellent, then we can all discuss what further actions will need to be taken later this afternoon."

We all adjourned to the restaurant, which was indeed excellent, and we continued to discuss ideas for a couple of hours. We eventually left Moory and Khalid around six o'clock, and headed back to the airport in the silver minibus, with Moory's promise that Dubai's police would clamp down on the brothers in every way they could, while at the same time talking to the Omanis about raiding the warehouses as soon as possible, and putting a permanent stop to the arms shipments. We all boarded the Gulfstream feeling pretty exhausted, and George took off with Colin alongside him in the co-pilot's seat, and the plane headed back to the UK while the rest of us all fell asleep.

Chapter Twenty-Five

After a late brunch the following day, we, that is Paul, Richard, Helena, George, Colin, Jo, Sam and myself, all reconvened in Stephen's office at Greenwich Police station. Kurt was back in Amsterdam and Paulo had returned to the Algarve the previous evening.

"While you were all off lazing about and sunning yourselves in Dubai," began Stephen, "Richard, Jo, Paulo and I have been doing some real police work, and we have come up with a plan for how to tackle our Faro Forger. I've already run it past Kurt and he is in total agreement."

"So," I asked, "are we going to trap him in a brilliant sting operation, catch him red handed and then lock him up in prison for the rest of his life?"

"No," replied Stephen. "We're going to recruit him."

"We're going to what?" exclaimed a thunderstruck Sam.

Stephen smiled at us all and continued.

"If we end up putting Cornelius Janssen in prison, he's going to be no use to us or to anybody else, and he just becomes another statistic and a massive cost to the state."

"Surely, he'd go to prison in Portugal though, not here?" I queried.

"Possibly," replied Stephen. "But you must already know this, Michael, as you live in Portugal. Paulo told me quite clearly that it takes years for cases to get to court, and half the time criminals end up walking away or doing a runner as they simply don't have enough prisons in Portugal to run an effective remand system. Paulo thinks we should try Janssen here for counterfeiting sterling, and then the court could take into consideration everything else he's done when sentencing."

"Sounds good to me," I said.

"Look, Michael," continued Stephen, "I read a report from the Justice department a few days ago, and it clearly stated that to lock up a prisoner in Strangeways for example costs the state £41,200 a year. Our Mr. Janssen would get a minimum sentence of 25 years for all his criminal activities, which will cost the British taxpayer over a million pounds."

"So, what are you suggesting?" asked Paul.

"Kurt and I are in full agreement on this. We, that is you two, Paul and Michael, go to the Algarve, with Paulo's blessing, find Janssen, get him on his own, and quietly take him to one side for a lengthy chat. You offer him the same deal Kurt offered Martin Smith six years ago. Immunity from all prosecution if he fills us in on everything to do with the Bukharis, plus, and this is an essential requirement of any deal, everyone else he knows of that is involved in the forgery business. He turns state evidence for us and stays out of prison, but only if he then works for Interpol for the foreseeable future. Given the choice of working for Kurt or spending the rest of his life in a concrete box with metal bars, I'm pretty sure he'll accept our proposal. If he doesn't, Paul will arrest him there and then and bring him back to the UK in handcuffs."

"How do we get to Faro?" Paul asked.

"George and Colin will fly you both out to the Algarve, while the rest of us continue to put information together that your friend Khalid can use against the Bukharis. Richard here is still coming up with information from your breaking and entering exploits..."

I decided to let his comment go this time.

"...and he says he will have a complete report ready by the end of the week."

"Any news from Kurt's team on the brothers' codes?" asked Sam.

"Yes," replied Richard. "As Stephen said, I should have the completed report soon, and that should include all the codes. Kurt's Arabic specialists have already broken most of the codes, and that has already given us a lot more information, but they say they need another day or so to work on the final Arabic codes. They are apparently far harder to crack."

"So, Paul," said Stephen, "can you and Michael please go back to the Algarve this afternoon, find Cornelius Janssen who is now back in the Algarve according to Richard's phone tracker, have a nice little chat with him, explain the facts of life to him and then bring the sod back here, either with or without handcuffs depending on his response?"

George and Colin flew with Paul and I to Faro that same afternoon, as some of the additional information obtained from the codes included details of Cornelius Janssen's mobile phone, and as Stephen had said, Richard could now track its location. He informed us that Janssen was currently in Almancil and appeared to be located in the print shop we'd raided previously. Well, his phone was in the print shop, and we just assumed he was with the phone. We now knew what Janssen looked like as the Dutch authorities had given Kurt a copy of his passport photograph, which showed a clean-shaven man with dark hair and a small pointed beard on his chin, but he could have course changed his appearance. We collected a small hire car from Faro airport where we also picked up Paulo, and then the three of us drove to the print shop on the outskirts of São Lourenço. About four o'clock, we parked up out of sight amongst the trees. We wanted to follow Janssen and catch him on his own without anyone else knowing. So, began the waiting game.

Several people left the print shop about six o'clock in the evening, but we continued to wait as Janssen was definitely not one of those who'd left. About seven thirty, two men came out together, one of whom we immediately recognized as Alexio Ribeiro. The other was definitely our man – Cornelius Janssen. They both got in the same car, a grey Land Rover Discovery, and drove off. Paul, who was driving our hired silver Opel Astra followed at a discreet distance behind. Before we'd left the UK, Richard had given us a small tracking device that showed us where Janssen's mobile phone was located, and this was very helpful as it showed his phone was in the Land Rover in front of us. It basically meant that even if we lost sight of them, we could find them again. As it happened, we didn't lose them as they drove through São Lourenço and into Almancil. They stopped outside a shop selling Jacuzzis and walked across the road and into a smart restaurant called 'The Vaults'. We waited in our parked car, and eventually they left the restaurant just before ten o'clock. We continued to follow them and Ribeiro, who was driving, eventually dropped off Janssen outside a nice-looking villa on the outskirts of Almancil. We waited for Ribeiro to disappear, got out of the car, locked it, walked up the path to

Aerial View of Faro Marina

Faro Marina

Janssen's front door and knocked. He opened it more or less straight away muttering to himself.

"What have you forgotten Alex?" he took one look at us and tried to slam the door in our faces. However, Paulo had already put his foot in the door and the slamming process had no effect on his heavy police boots other than to bounce the door back into Janssen's face. We all entered his villa and sat the startled forger down into one of his armchairs.

"Good evening Mr. Janssen," began Paulo. "Allow us to introduce ourselves. I am Inspector Paulo Cabrita of the Portuguese GNR, this gentleman is Detective Inspector Paul Naismith of London's Metropolitan police, and this gentleman is from Interpol."

We all produced our various IDs and briefly stuck them under his nose.

"We would like to have a word with you," continued Paulo, "about certain activities you have been involved in over the last few years."

"Please understand," said Paul taking over, "that for you, life has just changed forever. We have enough evidence against you, Alexio Ribeiro, Ahmed and Nudara Bukhari and all your printing workers to lock the lot of you up for the rest of your lives. You have been involved in the selling of arms to numerous terrorist organizations around the world, and we have several options as to what to do with you."

"That was nothing to do with me," Janssen pleaded. "I just printed a few documents for them. I didn't sell any arms to terrorists? Really, that was nothing to do with me."

"That was what most of the Nazi's said about the holocaust after the Second World War," responded Paul. "It didn't work then and it doesn't work now. You're as guilty as hell."

"We at Interpol," I said, joining in applying the pressure we were putting on him and as agreed beforehand, "do not take kindly to people who provide the means for terrorists to arm themselves with weapons such as sarin and mustard gas, both of which I'm sure you know are classified worldwide as weapons of mass destruction. One of the options open to us would simply be to hand you over to the authorities in one of the countries that has been affected by your deadly actions."

"The Mossad in Israel for example," said Paul.

"I promise you, Guantanamo Bay will be delighted to welcome you as a permanent new resident," I added. "The Arab terrorists still locked up there would, I'm sure, love to have nightly chats with you."

"Oh my God!" he said, and he shriveled up on his chair holding his head in his hands.

We now knew for certain that he was ours, and from then on would do whatever we asked.

"There is however an easier option," said Paul, and he then outlined our proposal.

After the lengthy explanation of what would be required from him and obtaining Janssen's agreement to play ball, Paul confiscated his mobile phone, his iPad, and a laptop; all found in his villa. We then allowed Cornelius Janssen to fill a suitcase with some of his clothes and toiletries, but only under supervision of course, and we then handcuffed him for ease of security and took him to Faro, where he joined George, Colin, Paul and I on the Gulfstream. Paulo left us at this point informing us that he and his men would take Ribeiro into custody immediately, and that first thing in the morning the GNR would arrest everyone at the print shop and confiscate every scrap of their equipment. The two Rolls Royce jet engines located on either side at the rear of the fuselage started up, and the Gulfstream G650ER soon soared into the night sky on the journey back to its base at Biggin Hill airport. On our arrival we were surprised to find Helena, Richard, Sam and Jo all there to meet us with a message from Stephen, and several suitcases. We should refuel the plane immediately, turn around and head to Dubai. Khalid had news and he needed us all there as soon as possible.

Chapter Twenty-Six

We landed in Dubai mid-morning their time and were met by Khalid.

"Good morning to all of you," he said. Paul introduced Richard and Jo who had not met Khalid previously and then we all climbed into two large people movers. We drove the short distance to police HQ where we went back to the same conference room where yet again Brigadier Murad El Hashem, or Moory as we now knew him was waiting for us.

"Ladies and gentlemen, welcome to Dubai once more," he began. "I won't waste time as there is none to waste. In your absence we have had two very productive meetings with the Omani authorities, and they are going to raid the Bukhari's three warehouses in strength this afternoon. All of you, along with Khalid and myself have been invited to attend and observe, providing none of you, and this is extremely important, none of you or us interfere in any way. Then after it is all over, we have all been invited to meet the Sultan at his palace in Muscat, so that he can personally thank you for all your hard work in this matter. The Sultan is very proud of his country and does not wish it to be associated with terrorism in any form. So, ladies and gentlemen, onwards and upwards as you British say, to the Sultanate of Oman to watch the Bukhari brothers get what's coming to them."

We flew to Oman on the Dubai police's own aircraft, namely two AgustaWestland AW169 ten seat helicopters. We landed at the edge of Muscat airport, out of sight of the main terminal building. We showed our passports to the customs officials, but we were all expected and our papers received no more than a cursory glance. We were met by Major General Tariq Khan of the Oman Army's ground forces. He introduced himself, asked us all to address him simply as General for simplicity, and he then took us in two dark green minibuses to the main terminal where he had a red and green tourist coach with a civilian driver parked just outside the airport's main entrance. He suggested we all board it, and sit quietly until he was able to join us on board and brief us. We casually walked out of the airport and got on to the coach, along with hundreds of other mostly western tourists who were also just like us, climbing onto their coaches. Sam and I sat together immediately behind Paul and Khalid.

"Well if the airport is being watched," said Paul, "they won't suspect anything from us. We look just like any other bunch of tourists with a few bags of hand luggage."

"What have George and Colin got in those rucksacks?" I asked Paul.

"No idea," he replied. "If you're that bothered, ask them."

I wasn't that bothered as they were seated several rows away, and it meant leaving my seat.

"Any idea what the plan is?" I asked Khalid.

"Sorry Michael, I haven't a clue," he answered.

"But I suspect Major General Khan will inform us all in due course."

"Do you know him well?" Sam asked leaning forward in her seat next to me.

"Yes," replied Khalid. "I've met him twice before and he is very good and extremely efficient. But please remember, he is army, not police, and they are used to using guns every day, and they'll use their guns on this operation without thinking twice, if required."

"Well I don't suppose the Bukhari brothers will want to come quietly," I said. "Even if they're asked really politely. They've survived this long, so they can't be totally stupid. They must realize all is not well in their world."

"Agreed," mused Khalid. "We know that they know they are in trouble because of all the restrictions we've put on them. We've frozen all their bank accounts, and every bank we've spoken to in seven different countries have all agreed to freeze their accounts with immediate effect until they hear directly from Brigadier Murad El Hashem."

"I bet that's pissed them off," mused Paul with a slight laugh.

"You can count on it," said Khalid. "But unfortunately it will have also tipped them off that they are under investigation. They need to shift all those weapons as soon as possible."

Muscat, the Capital of the Sultanate of Oman

Muscat at Night

“Do we know for sure they are all still in the warehouses?” asked Sam.

“Yes. The warehouses have been under 24 hours, 7 days a week surveillance since we told Major General Khan. He has over 30 men in the area, most working undercover as fork lift drivers, manual laborers, truck drivers etc.”

At that point Major General Khan climbed on to the coach with a younger man alongside him. He pulled the door shut and walked halfway down the coach towards us.

“Thank you all for your patience,”' he began, “and a warm welcome to you all. Now we know both brothers are currently inside the largest of the three warehouses, and my plan is very simple. As you can see, myself and Lieutenant Asif Hamid here are both dressed in plain western style clothes, although we are not stupid and we do have Kevlar vests on under our suits, just in case anyone decides to shoot at us. Our arrival at the front door should not unduly alarm anyone inside the warehouse, and we simply intend to ask to speak to Ahmed whom we believe to be the calmer of the two brothers. We will simply inform him that we know everything about their arms operation, and that we have them completely surrounded and that they should quietly surrender to the Omani armed forces and avoid any conflict.”

“Do you think they are likely to agree?” asked Paul.

“Highly unlikely I would think,” he replied, “But I have to make them the offer. Can I please stress once more the importance of you not getting involved in any way? There is a cliff above the industrial estate where the warehouses are located from which you will all be able to see what happens very clearly. Please wear these ID cards at all times so that my men know you are on the side of the angels, i.e. me.”

The General handed out laminated ID cards on the end of red and green striped lanyards to each of us, which we all put over our heads so that they hung down the front of our chests.

“I fear this could be extremely dangerous, and I don’t want to have any of your deaths on my conscience. Everyone OK with that?” he asked.

We all nodded and muttered our agreement after which he gave the go sign to the driver. The engine of the coach started, and we made our twenty-minute journey to the outskirts of the industrial estate. We arrived at a large car park out of site of the warehouses, and all clambered off the coach. We soon discovered why George had brought a rucksack and what was in it. He had brought all four pairs of the binoculars from the Gulfstream with him, and when we got to the edge of the ridge which looked down on the warehouse area, we all laid down on our stomachs and George distributed the binoculars, roughly one pair between three of us. I had Sam on my left and Richard on my right. Helena was, needless to say, alongside Richard, with Khalid and Paul just beyond them. The rest of our team were all spread out to my left.

I was watching the area through the binoculars and all seemed very quiet at the warehouse. About five minutes after our arrival, we saw Major General Khan and Lieutenant Hamid slowly approach the largest of the three warehouses. They were about ten feet from the blue painted steel front door when it suddenly burst open outwards. In the door frame stood Nudara Bukhari holding a machine pistol. He said nothing but simply shot the Lieutenant three times in the chest, and he then took aim at the General, who immediately dived sideways. Lieutenant Hamid went down under the impact, the door slammed shut after Nudara Bukhari had rushed back inside, and then all hell broke loose. Two men who had been cleaning cars nearby rushed over, and with the help of the General who had damaged his right arm when he dived, they scooped up Lieutenant Hamid and quickly carried him back behind one of the cars. The two cleaners were both in fact under cover soldiers, and they were wearing their uniforms under their overalls which they now removed. All over the now hectic industrial estate men were suddenly removing their overalls, dishdashas and other forms of disguise revealing their army uniforms underneath.

"Good move," muttered Khalid. "Now everyone knows exactly who's on which side."

Most were already wearing side arms, but there were obviously stashes of weapons all over the place. The Omani army were now firing machine guns through all the various windows of the warehouse and the noise was deafening, even from where we were on the ridge. A minute later an Omani armored personnel carrier with a large gun on the front rolled into the area in front of the warehouse and fired a shell at the front door of the warehouse. It missed the door but made a fair-sized hole in the white concrete wall alongside it.

A moment later, a window on the top floor suddenly swung open, and several soldiers seeing the movement fired through the window, but no one appeared to be hit. The soldiers on the personnel carrier were now standing up and just starting to dismount from the back of the truck when a bazooka shell shot out through the upstairs window and blew the personnel carrier, and everyone on it to bits. Not one of the twelve soldiers on board could have possibly survived as the vehicle's petrol tank exploded and then burst into flame. Sam grabbed me in horror at what she'd just witnessed and buried her face in my shoulder.

"God, this is awful Michael," she wailed. "I can't watch it any longer. Can we please leave and go back to the coach?"

Sam was of course my main concern and so I immediately agreed. We were about to leave when a round of machine gun shots from the warehouse flew over my head destroying the bush behind me.

"Keep down everyone," I yelled. "We've been spotted, and we're now under fire here. Crawl backwards, and for God's sake, all keep your heads right down."

Everyone did as suggested, and once we were back far enough we all raced down the hill to the safety of the coach, which now had a cordon of Omani troops surrounding it. General Khan and the two troops that had helped him scoop up Lieutenant Hamid had now made it back to the coach and the Lieutenant had been told by the General to stay put on the coach and rest. He was suffering from severe impact wounds, but the Kevlar vest had done its job and protected him and he would recover after rest. Jo, who had the most medical training out of all of us said she would look after him.

The General, who now had his right arm in a sling, quickly spun round and walked back to the door of the coach. I wanted a quick word before he left, so much to Sam's horror I got off the coach and followed about twenty feet behind him. We'd both passed through the cordon of Omani troops, and the General was slowly and carefully making his way back past several clumps of bushes on the outskirts of the industrial estate. I suddenly caught a glimpse of light flash to the right of the General, and I immediately realized it was the blade of a knife glinting in the sun. I shouted a warning to General Khan, but with all the noise of the explosions and the nonstop machine gun fire, he couldn't hear me. Now anyone will tell you, I'm not a particularly brave person, but I guess instinct just kicked in, and I ran straight at the man with the knife, launched myself through air and just about managed to grab his arm in time as he was bringing it down in order to stab the General in the back. Both myself and the Bukharis' man were now lying on the ground, and as General Khan both heard and felt the impact, he immediately spun round. He sized up the situation in a flash, pulled out his pistol and shot his would-be assailant in the head. The blood splattered over my face and my shoulder, and I immediately threw up. General Khan looked at me, shook his head and simply said,

"Thank You."

He then ran back to the industrial estate to take charge of what was happening there. I didn't want to return to the coach covered in blood, which would only upset Sam even more, so I quietly and tentatively followed the route the General had taken. He was now fully in charge again directing his troops who were still getting a battering from bazooka shells and machine gun fire. I kept well back from the action, but from my position behind a pile of wooden pallets I could see everything. Movement in the distance suddenly caught my attention and one thing I did notice that nobody else appeared to have seen, was that Ahmed Bukhari had somehow managed to sneak out of the back door of the furthest warehouse and was now quickly heading towards one of the Iranian speedboats tied up at the far end of the dock from where they ran their smuggling operation. Ahmed was carrying a silver colored metal briefcase in his left hand and what looked like a Heckler and Koch MP5 sub machine gun in his right. I wasn't going to tackle a man carrying an MP5, but I did manage to attract the attention of one of the Omani troops, whose immediate reaction was to point his machine gun at me as I was not wearing a uniform. I raised my left arm and held up my ID tag with my right, then pointed to the speedboats and the fleeing Ahmad Bukhari. He cottoned on straight away and beckoned me over towards him. I bent low and ran over to him.

"Come with me." He said and took me straight to the General.

“You again?” the General spluttered. “Are you trying to get yourself killed?” he demanded.

“Never mind that,” I responded. “Ahmed Bukhari has somehow got out through the back of the end warehouse, and he’s making a run for it in one of the Iranian speedboats.”

“Damn and blast the man. I wish I could bomb the place, but there’s so much armament and toxic gas in there I could end up killing half the population of Oman.” He pulled out his radio and spoke very quickly in Arabic.

“Come with me,” he said. “I need you where I can see you. It appears to be the only way I can guarantee your safety, and like it or not, I owe you. But please, for everyone’s sake do what I say for once. Understood?”

“Yes, General,” I meekly replied.

We ran behind the piles of pallets, oil drums and bushes back towards the smaller car park, not the main car park where our coach was parked. Just as we arrived a matt black NH Industries NH90 military helicopter was landing. I only recognized it because Khalid had told me earlier all about the range of equipment the Omanis had at their disposal.

“Get on board, sit behind me, fasten your seat belt and keep quiet,” instructed the General. I did what I was told.

The helicopter took off and headed towards the open sea. Both of its side doors had been slid forward and we could now see the speedboat skipping over the sea at a tremendous rate of knots through the open doors. The pilot and co-pilot in the front were engrossed in their work, and in the back section was just the General, the helicopters navigator, one sharp shooter soldier armed with a submachine gun and me. The General put on his headset and spoke into the microphone.

“Fly over him, turn and hover in front of him so that we can get a shot off. I want that bastard alive if at all possible.”

The pilot did as instructed and the sharp shooter beside me carefully lined up his shot. Unfortunately, Ahmed Bukhari wasn’t worried about carefully lining up a shot, and he simply raked the helicopter from his MP5 just before our sharpshooter got his shot away.

Only two of the bullets entered the helicopter, but one hit the sharpshooter in the shoulder just where he rests his weapon, and he immediately dropped the rifle on the floor and fell backwards.

The other shot hit the ceiling of the helicopter showering us both with a mixture of glass fiber and shards of metal, one of which cut the Generals head.

"Shoot the bastard," yelled the General at me.

"I can't as I've got my firing arm in a bloody sling. It's either you shoot him or he gets away."

The pilot had lifted the helicopter higher and dropped back behind the fleeing speedboat. I gingerly picked up the rifle, which was far heavier than I'd anticipated.

"Push the butt into deep into your shoulder," the General said. "It's got a hell of a recoil if you're not used to it. Aim at the center of his body and then squeeze, don't pull the trigger, gently squeeze it."

"I'll try," I said. "But I'm a travel and crime writer, not a bloody soldier."

"Just aim for his chest. Even if you miss that you might hit him somewhere which should at least slow him down a bit. We've got to stop him entering Iranian waters."

The helicopter swung round again and picking up speed it moved alongside the speedboat, but about fifty feet above it. Bukhari had to try and watch where he was steering with one hand while trying to shoot at us with the other. The MP5 was just too heavy for him to operate properly with one hand and his shots went well wide. I did as I'd been instructed by the General and aimed at Ahmed's chest and gently squeezed the trigger. The powerful rifle, an American Colt M4A1 Carbine with ACOG optic was using explosive bullets and the rifle kicked back into my shoulder. The bloody thing shot out of my hands, bounced on the floor of the helicopter and fell out of the open door. Although I had aimed at his chest, the kick back was far more than I had been expecting and my shots had been off by about three feet. The sharp shooter had set the rifle up on three bullet bursts, but I hadn't known that. The first shot had missed completely, however the second went straight through the outboard engine attached to the back, but even more spectacularly the third shot hit the large can of spare fuel lying on the floor of the speedboat. Because the rifle had been loaded with explosive bullets there was an almighty explosion and both Ahmed Bukhari and his speedboat disintegrated in a ball of flame, flesh and flying metal. The General just looked at me in either horror or sympathy for my ineptitude – I couldn't tell which – and then he just burst out laughing.

The helicopter turned and started to head back as the co-pilot informed the General that the situation at the warehouses was now under control and they'd managed to take Nudara Bukhari alive. We landed in the larger car park next to our coach, and we both climbed down from the machine looking a right state. The General had his right arm in a sling and his face was covered with blood running down from his head wound where the shard of metal had cut into his forehead and was still lodged there. I was still covered in the blood splatter from earlier, plus a few extra cuts and some of my own blood from the metal shards. We both looked terrible, but we were in fact both fine.

Sam and the others all rushed over seeing us get off the helicopter, and Sam started hitting me with her fists, but only gently.

"Don't you ever do that to me again," she cried. "I thought I'd lost you."

"Well I'm glad he did," said the General. "Michael has saved my life twice in the last half hour or so, and without him Ahmed Bukhari would have escaped to Iran. So, don't be too harsh with him."

"I don't care," said Sam. "Promise me you'll never do that again."

"I promise," I replied. "I'll never do that again."

I felt fairly safe making the promise, as I thought the chances of me firing a sharpshooter's rifle in anger from a military helicopter chasing an arms dealer on his way to Iran in a speedboat were pretty remote.

Chapter Twenty-Seven

We were all staying in the amazing Shangri-La's Barr Al Jissah Resort and Spa hotel in Muscat. Later that evening, we had all been invited to the Sultan's palace in Muscat. It was a very formal affair at which various senior diplomats, civil servant types, military leaders and all of us were invited to the banquet which was to be hosted by the Sultan himself. We had no smart clothes with us, and Khalid suggested that he and Jo quickly take a note of all our measurements, which they did, and then Khalid telephoned the whole lot through to a good friend of his back in Dubai. Ninety minutes later his friend arrived by private jet, and he had on board a selection of Western clothes, all in our sizes. There were dinner jackets, black trousers, black shoes, white shirts and bow ties for all the men, and some absolutely beautiful Arabian-style silk dresses for all the ladies. I have to say, if you want to see real service in action, Dubai is the place to go. A stream of black Mercedes limousines pulled up outside our hotel and Khalid, who had arranged everything on our behalf, insisted that just two people got into the back of each one. Moory and Khalid were in the first car, followed by Sam and myself. Helena and Richard came next followed by George and Colin. Jo was very happily sharing her limousine with Paul.

After a wonderful meal, Major General Tariq Khan, Moory, Khalid and all of us from the UK were asked to go forward and stand in a line in front of all the other guests. The General was still supporting his arm in a sling, although this one was much more attractive than the previous blood-soaked version. We were all wondering why we'd all been asked to line up before the Sultan, and then a very smart man came forward and stood to one side of the Sultan. He then addressed the entire room in perfect English on behalf of the Sultan.

"My very good friends and colleagues, it is my profound wish as the Sultan of Oman to thank and honor these good people lined up before you, who have all acted bravely in the pursuit of honesty and justice, and in helping our own armed forces to restore peace to an extremely grateful nation. It is to that end that I as Sultan wish to bestow the Sultan's Gallantry Medal for supreme acts of gallantry in the face of the enemy, to every one of these people lined up here before you."

The Sultan then stepped forward, and with two attractive ladies holding blue cushions with all the medals laid out on them, the Sultan then proceeded down the line pinning a medal on the clothing of each of us, and thanking each of us personally in perfect English for all we had done on behalf of Oman. Sam as usual was standing next to me, and I was the very last in the line, as had been insisted upon much earlier by the Sultan's assistant. The Sultan's assistant then spoke again.

"If you could all kindly return to your seats please with our nation's great thanks."

He continued,

"With the exception that is of Major General Tariq Khan and Mr. Michael Turner."'

I wondered what on earth I had done wrong to be singled out, then I realized, I'd probably got the General into trouble by not following his orders and I was about to be punished, or at the very least reprimanded for getting him shot.

The Sultan stepped forward and this time he spoke himself.

"Earlier today, the much-loved leader of our armed forces Major General Tariq Khan and Mr. Michael Turner here faced untold danger, as did many others. However, unlike the brave men of our armed forces, Mr. Turner is not an Omani, nor was he being paid to defend Oman, nor was he asked to do what he did. What he in fact did do today was, as the British say, 'way above and beyond the call of duty', and indeed, twice today Mr. Turner saved the life of Major General Tariq Khan, on both occasions risking his own life in order to do so. Both General Khan and I are extremely grateful, and I, as the Sultan of Oman wish to recognize your brave and gallant actions, and therefore, I present to you Mr. Michael Turner the highest honor our nation can award, 'The Most Honorable Order of Oman'. I have to tell you Mr. Turner that this award is the Omani equivalent of being awarded a knighthood in your own country, and so any time you are in Oman you will from now on be referred to as Sir Michael.

You and your family are welcome in Oman as honored guests at the palace any time you may wish to visit our grateful nation."

The Sultan stepped forward and hung the order around my neck, a chain of white gold and diamonds with a gold and white enamel medal hanging beneath it on a red ribbon with green edges. In addition, he pinned a six-pointed star on my breast pocket, again in gold and white enamel with a green and red circular badge at its center. To say I was overcome would be an understatement. First the Sultan shook my hand and then the General did the same, thanking me once again for my actions. The Sultan approached me again and said quietly so that nobody else could hear,

"I suspect you would like nothing better than to go and sit down as soon as possible Mr. Turner. I don't think you like being up here in the limelight, so you would hate my job. Why don't you go and sit next to your lovely fiancée and get on with sorting out a date for your wedding, which I would be truly honored to attend – if I was to be invited."

The Sultan smiled at me once more, shook my hand again and then left me to return to my seat as he walked over to talk to Major General Khan. I went and sat down next to Sam where I was immediately surrounded by the rest of the team who were all admiring my 'Most Honorable Order of Oman'.

"I'm so very proud of you Michael," whispered Sam in my ear.

"The Sultan has told me we have to get on with setting a date for the wedding," I whispered back, "so that he can book it into his diary. He said he would be honored to attend, if he was to be invited."

"Well I guess we better agree a date fast," smiled Sam. "Then it all depends if there's room to squeeze him onto the guest list." And we both laughed.

Epilogue

We stayed in Oman relaxing at the hotel for another two days, and then we all flew back to the UK on Interpol's Gulfstream. On the plane we chatted about all sorts of things, and Paul told us he'd now received a lot of additional information from Khalid.

"Apparently," Paul said, "they discovered two concrete-lined tunnels dug by the brothers, although not personally dug by them I suspect, between the three warehouses, and then in addition a much longer one going out to the edge of the docks. That's how Ahmed managed to get out to the speedboat without being seen by the troops. They all assumed everybody was trapped inside, and it never occurred to anyone that there might be escape tunnels. Thank God, you spotted him."

"What happened to all the armaments in the end?" asked Sam.

"We're shipping them all back to Interpol headquarters in Lyon," replied Helena, "where everything will be logged and catalogued, and then we'll pass the whole lot onto United Nations Enforcement, who will eventually destroy the lot. They have the means of safely disposing of everything, including the mustard and sarin gases."

"And what's going to happen to Nudara Bukhari?" asked Jo.

"Ah, well, that particular gentleman has changed his tune and his attitude. The minute he discovered his brother was dead, he decided that he'd been totally duped by his brother and he was completely innocent in the whole affair. It was Ahmed who did all the arms deals, killed people if they got in the way etc. Nudara claims he was merely the accountant / bookkeeper who thought he was dealing with agricultural machinery."

"Oh, well that seems quite reasonable," I responded.

"I can only assume that was a piece of agricultural machinery. I'm not familiar with what he used to shoot

Lieutenant Asif Hamid with?" I asked. "Or has that little misdemeanor slipped his mind?"

"Oh, that," replied Paul. "The stupid idiot claims his brother put the machine gun in his hands and then shoved him out of the door. He claims it was simply self-defense. Kill or be killed, if you please."

"So, what will happen to him?" repeated Jo.

"He'll probably get life in prison," answered Paul.

"So, he won't be executed?" asked Sam.

"Unlikely," he replied. "The Omanis used to have a terrible reputation for human rights," said Paul, "as their law was based on Islamic Sharia law, but it has undoubtedly improved over the last few years. The last known execution in Oman was way back in 2001, and as far as we know there is no one under sentence of death in the Omani prison system. Nudara Bukhari will be tried in court. He will undoubtedly be found guilty and sentenced. He will most likely receive life in an Omani prison. To be quite honest, I'm not sure if I wouldn't prefer the death penalty if it were me. Life in prison in that heat and humidity, no thank you, I couldn't hack it."

"Any news from Portugal on our Faro Forger?" asked Helena.

"Oh yes, there's lots to tell, but Stephen would skin me alive and send me back to face life in that Omani prison if I didn't let him fill you in. Sorry, but you'll have to wait."

Once we'd arrived back in the UK, we decided not to meet until the following day so that we could all have a refreshing shower, a change of clothes, a meal, a good night's rest, a hearty breakfast and then all be wide awake for a ten o'clock meeting. We all arrived at Greenwich police station and as Sam and I walked through the door, the Desk Sergeant Don Priestly greeted us both.

"Good morning, Sir Michael, and I assume Lady Samantha. It is so kind of you to grace this, our most humble dwelling place with your gracious and omnipotent presence."

"Sod off, Don," I replied, "or I'll have you beheaded."

"Thank you, Don," laughed Sam, "but please, don't encourage him. It will only go to his head, and he's already totally insufferable as it is."

The Sultan of Oman's Yacht

The Most Honourable Order of Oman

Don laughed as he picked up the phone to let Stephen know we'd all arrived.

"Seriously Michael," said Don returning the phone, "well done mate and good on you."

"Thanks Don, but I only did what any of the others would have done if they'd found themselves in my situation."

"Very true," said Stephen from behind us, who had just arrived from his office. The difference is, Michael, you actually did it. They may well have, but you actually did, so well done. Come through all of you. Kurt is with us having flown in from Amsterdam last night and Paulo arrived on the early morning flight from Faro, so we've got a full house. Don, can you organize tea and biscuits for us all please."

"Yes boss," replied Don, and we all walked through into Stephen's office.

There was lots of handshaking and hugs as everybody greeted Kurt and Paulo, and after the tea and biscuits had been brought in we all squeezed around Stephen's conference table.

"OK everyone," stated Stephen, "I'll try not to make this a monologue, but there is a lot of information to share with you all. Firstly, our Faro Forger, Mr. Cornelius Janssen, has been singing like a canary, and I'll hand straight over to Kurt who has him caged in Amsterdam."

"Good morning everyone, and well done all of you. OK. Our Mr. Janssen, and yes, he is now well and truly ours. It was Paul and Michael, if you'll pardon the expression that really scared the shit out of him. It was your suggestion that we might send him to spend the rest of his life in Guantanamo Bay that really swung it, Michael. Nice touch. Anyway, the first thing he gave us was the names of everyone he knew in the Faro operation. I then fed all those names through to Paulo who has been busy rounding them up. Paulo?"

"Yes, thank you Kurt," said Paulo. "Janssen gave us twenty-six names in total. That included printers, four drivers, laborers to move paper stocks and ink around etc. and several heavies, as well as Alexio Ribeiro whom we knew about already. We have rounded up twenty-five of them and we now have them all held on remand in Faro prison. The only one we haven't been able to find yet is a man named Kristof Pavlov, a Greek heavy who worked for Ribeiro. We think he may have 'done a runner' as you British say, and headed back to Crete. Ribeiro himself is also in Faro prison on remand, and they will all be there for quite a while as their court cases aren't scheduled to start until early next year. I'm afraid Justice in Portugal can be very slow, but in this instance, I'm in no hurry."

"Excellent Paulo," exclaimed Stephen, "'and thank you for all your help. Now over to you again Kurt for news of the various missing yachts."

"Before I start on that," said Kurt. "I would like to point out that Alexio Ribeiro will eventually be extradited to Greece, but only under very tightly controlled Interpol supervision. Once, he's back in Crete he will join all his criminal brethren in one of Crete's beautiful prisons. We believe we have them all now, and Ribeiro with be joining them once the extradition order comes through. Now, as Stephen said, I have news on the various stolen yachts. The 'Nefertiti' that you last saw disappearing into the mouth of the cave off the island of Crete reappeared a week later with its hull now painted pure white with a green coach line running the full length, whereas the hull was dark blue when it disappeared. It now has twin raked funnels in cream, which again is different from its original dark blue cylindrical funnel. There are also some extra stainless-steel railings here and there, and finally it is no longer called the 'Nefertiti', and it has now been renamed the 'Cretan Odyssey' would you believe? And just for fun it flies a Panamanian flag."

"Where is it now?" asked George.

"I can answer that one," said Richard who brought two images up on to the large TV monitor at the end of the table. The left-hand image was a map with a red dot flashing on and off, and the right hand image a crisp color photograph."

"It's currently docked in the harbor at Valletta in Malta, its position is shown by the flashing red dot. The picture on the right is what the 'Nefertiti' now looks like and that was taken two hours ago by an Interpol operative and Kurt had it sent over to us."

"Well I'd never have recognized it if I didn't know," exclaimed Colin. "And I saw the 'Nefertiti' up close in Crete. Give the bastards their due, they've done a great job."

"So great in fact," said Kurt, "'that Pieter Van Riesbrink, who if you remember is the yacht's owner, has seen that particular photograph and says he now prefers how the yacht looks to its original dark blue. We have a team of four operatives taking possession of the yacht later this morning, and the Maltese police are going to hold the pirate crew in one of their jails until we decide what to do with them."

"Any news on any of the other yachts?" asked Helena.

"We've got them all located, apart from two which we are still working on. The information you guys obtained on the Bukharis' computers in Dubai provided most of the information we needed. The 'Princess Sophie' is already back with its owner, and he is having it put back into its original color scheme and name. We got a quote for the work from the original shipyard in Port Townsend, and we have agreed to cover the cost from the funds confiscated from the Bukharis' accounts."

"What's happening to all their money?" asked Sam.

"Kurt and I sat and discussed it at length," said Stephen, "once we knew exactly how much we were actually dealing with. Between all the various accounts there were over 12 billion US dollars, which if you remember was spread among numbered bank accounts in the Caymans, the Bahamas, Belize, Switzerland, Lebanon, Monaco and Singapore."

"Thanks to all of you and your burglary skills," said Kurt, "we had all the account numbers, passwords etc., and so we simply emptied all their accounts and transferred everything into a new Interpol Client account. Some will be transferred to the people that had property stolen or were duped with counterfeit, but that amounts to less than a third."

"We decided what we ideally wanted to do with what was left of the confiscated money, approximately 8 billion US dollars," continued Stephen, "was to distribute it amongst worthy causes, but first, we approached the only two governments that might feel they had a legitimate claim to it."

"As we suspected they would," said Kurt, "they both gave us the green light to redistribute the Bukharis' ill-gotten gains amongst twelve excellent international charities, who will all get a sudden boost of approximately six hundred million US dollars each."

"They are," listed Stephen, "The Red Cross, the Red Crescent, Médecins Sans Frontières, UNICEF, The United Nations Foundation, Oxfam, Save the Children, Compassion

International, The International Medical Corps, Children in Need, Samaritan's Purse and World Medical Relief."

"Wow, that is amazing," said Sam. "And nobody objected?"

"Well as Stephen said," replied Kurt, "the only countries that had a possible claim on it would have been the UAE and Oman, as those are the two countries where the brothers operated from. Both the UAE's ruling Council and Michael's new best friend, the Sultan of Oman were more than happy for us to use the money in this way. Let's be honest here, neither of their countries really needed the money, and I think they were more than happy with our decisions.'

"So, what do we do now?" I asked.

"Well, I suppose you two better book a date for your wedding," said Stephen. "Most of us here are very busy people, and if you want us all there, which we obviously hope you do, then can I suggest you get on with it and let us all know as soon as possible."

"I actually meant regarding the case, not the wedding," I protested. But it was to no avail. The case was over, well at least as far as we were concerned, and so Sam and I sat down that evening to choose a date for our wedding. We decided we didn't want a big flash affair, so we opted not to wait but to get on with it.

Two months later Sam walked down the aisle, looking absolutely beautiful and radiant on Stephen's arm. Her dad had passed away several years earlier, long before I'd even met Sam, and so she had asked Stephen to give her away. Richard stood alongside me at the front as my best man, and Helena and Jo escorted Sam down the aisle as her two bridesmaids. Paul, George, Colin, Paulo, Kurt and Martin, who had flown over from South Africa for the occasion, all took on the role of ushers and we all had a glorious day. I thought afterwards that the most important people in our lives now were all in some way or another associated with crime, either internationally through Interpol, Portugal's GNR, or London's Metropolitan police.

Our guest of honor did keep to his word, and the Sultan of Oman flew to Faro on his private jet totally unannounced, and he and his two bodyguards sat quietly in the church along with everybody else. We had a wonderful service followed by an equally great evening at one of the Algarve's prestigious golf resorts, in which we had hired and taken over the bar and the restaurant for the festivities. Later that evening myself and the new Mrs. Turner left the reception, drove to Faro, boarded the Sultan's private jet and flew back to Oman with him. The Sultan had, as his wedding gift, very generously offered us the use of his private yacht and crew for the next two weeks. Needless to say, we had said a very big yes, and an even bigger thank you.

Later that night, as Sam and I sat in beautifully cushioned loungers on the top deck of the Sultan's yacht, cruising out to sea, we decided; it's good to have friends in high places.

THE END

Michael, Sam, Helena and Co will all return in The Salzburg Suicides – Book Three of the Algrave Crime Thrillers.